Rather than doing the smart thing and backing away from him, she took a step forward.

"Roxie," Luke said, his voice low in warning. "Be sure before you start something you'll regret later."

"I'm not starting anything," she said, and knew it was the truth. "I'm finishing it. Call it closure, call it once more for old time's sake...call it whatever you want. I'm going to call it the goodbye kiss I never got."

Working methodically when her hands wanted to shake and her pulse wanted to race, not even entirely sure what had gotten into her, Roxanne slipped off her gloves. Then she got him by one lab coat lapel in each hand and used that purchase to rise up onto her toes as his eyes went dark and her own blood heated.

He moved as she did, and they met halfway.

And kissed goodbye.

JESSICA ANDERSEN

WITH THE M.D....
AT THE ALTAR?

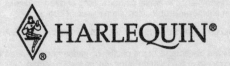
HARLEQUIN®

TORONTO • NEW YORK • LONDON
AMSTERDAM • PARIS • SYDNEY • HAMBURG
STOCKHOLM • ATHENS • TOKYO • MILAN • MADRID
PRAGUE • WARSAW • BUDAPEST • AUCKLAND

Special thanks and acknowledgment to
Jessica Andersen for her contribution to
The Curse of Raven's Cliff miniseries.

ISBN-13: 978-0-373-69335-1
ISBN-10:   0-373-69335-4

WITH THE M.D....AT THE ALTAR?

www.eHarlequin.com

Printed in U.S.A.

ABOUT THE AUTHOR

Though she's tried out professions ranging from cleaning sea lion cages to cloning glaucoma genes, from patent law to training horses, Jessica is happiest when she's combining all these interests with her first love: writing romances. These days she's delighted to be writing full-time on a farm in rural Connecticut that she shares with a small menagerie and a hero named Brian. She hopes you'll visit her at www.JessicaAndersen.com for info on upcoming books, contests and to say 'hi'!

Books by Jessica Andersen

CAST OF CHARACTERS

Roxanne Peterson—After giving up relief medicine for a place to call home, Rox never expects to find herself handling an outbreak in her hometown of Raven's Cliff... or needing the help of the man who broke her heart.

Luke Freeman—The hotshot toxicologist has his dream job leading a CDC outbreak team, but this is the first time he's been called on to handle a town overrun by both an outbreak and a two-hundred-year-old curse. Will his toughest case yet cost the life of the woman he once loved?

Perry Wells—The mayor wants the best for the residents of Raven's Cliff...or does he?

Bug Dufresne—Luke's teammate may be key to figuring out what is making the town's residents sick—and why some of them simply become ill while others become murderous.

Patrick Swanson—The chief of police is fighting a losing battle against a serial killer, a missing woman and a deadly outbreak. Maybe the town truly is cursed.

Theodore Fisher—The eccentric businessman has offered to lift the curse by restoring the old, burned-out Beacon Lighthouse. How is he connected to the mysterious caller pressuring the mayor to sell him the property?

May O'Malley—When Luke's teammate becomes ill, he's forced to face some hard truths about himself...and his past.

The Seaside Strangler—This fanatic killer believes that sacrificing a woman to the sea gods lifted the town's curse five years earlier. Now he must kill again to save Raven's Cliff.

The well-dressed man—He keeps an injured, unconscious woman in the caves beneath Beacon Lighthouse. What is he after?

Chapter One

Overtired, overworked and frustrated beyond belief, Dr. Roxanne Peterson pressed her cheek to the cool glass door of her small-town clinic. Even after nearly seventy-two hours of fighting the mysterious illness that had overtaken isolated Raven's Cliff, Maine, she still couldn't believe her town was in the throes of a deadly outbreak.

And it *was* her town, whether or not the intransigent locals accepted her as one of them rather than a newcomer.

She'd chosen this place, these people, despite the seaside town's remote location, nearly perpetual overcast gloom and the curse that supposedly haunted the area. Honestly, she'd chosen Raven's Cliff partly *because* of those things, and because her years of relief medicine in third-world countries had made her want to settle down somewhere, amidst people who needed her.

She'd never expected to be thrust back into desperate working conditions in Raven's Cliff, fighting a mysterious deadly disease with too little help and not enough equipment or supplies.

Yet that was exactly what was happening, she thought on a long sigh, looking through the glass door of the clinic to the world beyond.

It was pitch-black and raining outside, and thick fog made it difficult to see the shops lining the main street of the seaside town, which led to the town square on one side, the boardwalk and fishing docks on the other.

In past years, even this late on a rainy night, a few locals and tourists would have been window-shopping, exclaiming over the moored fishing boats, or leaning over the cliffside railing to catch a faceful of sea spray from the breakers that pounded the rocky Maine coastline.

There was nobody out tonight, though. Not with death stalking the streets of the quaint fishing village in the form of a strange disease...and what it made its victims become.

The locals were calling it the Curse, referring to a local legend about the town's sea-captain founder. Rox didn't put much stock in curses, but the disease certainly had terrifying consequences. Some patients became seriously ill. Others went psychotic.

Thinking of the things that'd happened over the past few days, Rox shivered as she stared out into the rain. During her five years in medical relief work, she'd seen her share of infectious outbreaks and environmental poisonings, yet she couldn't detect any pattern in this disease. The townspeople were getting sick without apparent rhyme or reason, with symptoms that didn't match any known disease and had so far proved impervious to the broad-spectrum antibiotics and antivirals she'd tried in the way of treatment.

At the moment she was fighting a rearguard action

with supportive, symptom-based therapies. Worse, she didn't have enough manpower to do the work that needed to be done. Her two full-time staff members had been among the first to get sick, and the other local doctor, who filled in for her when she needed help, was out of the country. Worse, the local hospitals—the closest of which was some forty miles away—were refusing to take patients from Raven's Cliff, and had barred their doctors from entering the town.

She couldn't blame the hospital administrators for their decision. In fact, she supported it. With only one road leading into the town, and the only other access from the sea, the town was eminently suitable for a lockdown quarantine that would keep the disease from escaping and spreading to other portions of the state, while the experts worked to identify, contain and cure the disease.

Unfortunately, she was currently the only expert in town, and she was running out of steam.

She was working flat-out trying to keep her patients alive, treating individual symptoms rather than the illness itself because she had no idea what was causing a flu-like disease in some patients, and violent rage in others. Were the townspeople infected with something? Were they being poisoned? Was it some sort of allergin? An environmental toxin? She had no idea, and she was nearly dead on her feet trying to keep up with the work.

She couldn't stop now, though. The death toll was up to four, the eight clinic beds were full with nonviolent patients and three of the violent patients were currently locked in the basement of the Raven's Cliff Town Hall, in the RCPD jail.

With no response yet from the plea for help she'd sent the Center for Disease Control, she was on her own.

Tears threatened—grief for the dead, for the dying. For herself and the fact that she felt completely, utterly alone in the town where she'd spent the two happiest years of her bounced-around childhood.

"Knock it off," she said aloud, hearing the words echo in the waiting room. "Feeling sorry for yourself isn't going to change a thing. Getting some sleep might."

Sometimes her subconscious did a better job than her waking self when it came to shuffling puzzle pieces into place. Besides, she was so tired she was going to start making mistakes soon if she didn't catch a few hours of downtime.

Forcing herself to push away from the clinic door, she flipped the sign from Open to Closed, though that was a formality since she was on constant call. Then she flicked off the lights, plunging the waiting room into darkness. She was just about to head upstairs to her apartment when she saw movement outside.

She stopped and stared through the clear glass door, trying to make out details through the fog.

Was someone there? She could've sworn she'd just seen a figure slip from the porch to the shadows beside the fog-cloaked building diagonally across the street.

Maybe it's a dog, she thought when she didn't see the motion again. *Or a raccoon. A deer.* Heck, even a bear would be preferable to what her gut told her she'd seen: a human figure hiding in the shadows long after the 8:00 p.m. curfew that Captain Patrick Swanson, the chief of police, had issued earlier that day.

Rox's instincts told her to call the cops to investigate. Under normal circumstances she never would've bothered them with something so mundane…but these were far from normal circumstances. Sure, it might be an animal, or teenagers refusing to let the curfew spoil the start of their summer fun. Then again, it was possible that Captain Swanson's last house-to-house sweep had missed seeing the red-tinged eyes and faintly jaundiced skin tones that were the only warning signs before the disease hit full-force.

Better to call the cops and have it be a raccoon than have a new Violent on the loose, Rox thought.

That was what the townspeople were calling the patients whose symptoms leaned toward psychosis: Violents. More accurately, as far as Rox could tell, they became uninhibited. The good tendencies in their personalities decreased and their negative sides took over, amplifying their normally controllable impulses and making them uncontrollable.

Of the four dead, only two had died from the disease itself. The other two had been murdered by one of the Violents. The threat of more such cases had left the townspeople locking their doors tight, and watching each other with grave suspicion. *Are you getting sick,* everyone was thinking. *Am I?*

Knowing she was far better making the call than not, Rox turned the lights back on and headed for the phone on the waiting room desk. She was halfway there when someone knocked on the glass door.

Her heartbeat kicked into overdrive as she turned and looked back. The glare of the lights reflecting on the glass panel meant she could only make out the indistinct figure of a man outside her door. She couldn't tell who it was. More importantly, she couldn't see his eyes or skin.

Training and compassion told her to answer the door in case someone needed her. Logic said she should wait for the cops.

Logic won, but just as she grabbed the phone, the man outside kicked his way in.

Rox screamed when the safety glass spiderwebbed and shattered inward.

Fingers trembling, she stabbed 9-1-1 on the phone. "It's Roxanne. I need help!"

It took her a second to realize the phone line was dead.

The wind howled through the broken door and driving rain spattered against the figure of local fisherman Aztec Wheeler as he stepped through the door.

He'd gotten the nickname Aztec from his straight, dark hair, sharp features and prominent nose, and his take-no-prisoners style on the high school basketball court. But this wasn't the easygoing young jock Rox had known in school, and it wasn't the grown man who'd asked her out twice since she'd come back to town and opened the clinic. This was someone else entirely.

Or rather, some*thing* else.

Aztec's dark hair was plastered to his skull and he was soaked to his yellow-tinged skin, but he didn't seem to notice the discomfort—his attention was locked on Rox, and his reddish eyes were hard with anger. With rage.

Smiling terribly, he lunged across the waiting room and grabbed her.

Panicked, Rox screamed and thrashed, trying to

break free from his grappling arms. She elbowed him in the ribs, but he twisted, putting his face near hers. It took her a terrified moment to realize he was actually trying to *kiss* her.

"Stop!" She shoved at him, but he was an immovable wall of muscle. "I said *stop!*"

"You should've said yes." His clothes were soaked and cold, but his skin and breath were fever-hot. "You shouldn't have turned me down like that."

Her panicked brain made the connection. He'd been interested in her, had asked her out a couple of times and she'd said no. Now, the Curse had warped his brain, turning a harmless crush into an obsession and loosening his normal control over his emotions.

She braced her forearm against his collarbone and pushed away, trying to reason with him, trying to talk to the man she knew him to be. "Listen to me, Aztec. You're sick. You don't really want to do this, the Curse is making you—"

He got his lips on her ear, but instead of kissing her he bit down, hard.

Pain lanced and Rox screamed, then screamed again when he yanked at her white doctor's coat, tearing the buttons and leaving the garment hanging half off her. Panic-stricken, she kneed him in the crotch, praying he would feel it.

Aztec doubled over with a howl.

Sobbing, Rox yanked away and bolted for the broken front door. She slipped and almost went down on the rain-slicked threshold, but kept going, running into the darkness.

The rain slashed at her, soaking through her clothes within seconds as she fled through the nearly impenetrable fog, headed for the town hall and the RCPD entrance around the side of the building.

The air smelled of the sea, thick and salty. Thunder grumbled in the distance and the wind howled like a living thing.

Rox ran for her life. Tears mingled with the rain on her face as Aztec's footsteps slapped on the wet pavement too close behind her. He howled something that might have been her name, and she realized she wasn't going to make it to the police station before he caught up.

No! she screamed inwardly. She put her head down and pushed harder, her legs burning as she pounded up the street.

Aztec closed on her. He grabbed her white coat, but she pulled free and kept going. She had to keep going, had to—

She saw headlights pause at a cross street up ahead. They turned toward her, creating bright halos in the thick fog.

Heart jammed in her throat, Rox waved her arms and ran into the light. *"Help me!"*

For half a second nothing happened, as if the driver didn't see her—or more likely couldn't believe what he was seeing. Then the big black SUV accelerated toward her with a roar. When it was nearly on top of her, the driver slammed on the brakes, slapped the transmission into Park and lunged out of the vehicle, snapping to his companions inside the big car. One of them tossed something to him, and he caught it and spun toward Roxanne, shouting, "Hit the deck!"

Though she couldn't see his face through the fog, the sound of his voice instantly kicked her back two years, to another epidemic on another continent. Another lifetime.

"Down!" he barked, and she obeyed automatically, throwing herself onto the wet pavement just as Aztec grabbed her hair. His wet fingers slipped and she fell free.

Something hissed over her head and hit Aztec with a sizzling thump. Seconds later, electricity jolted through Rox as the Taser's 50,000-volt charge transmitted through Aztec and across the wet pavement, giving her an unpleasant shock.

Aztec, though, bore the full brunt of the blast. He gurgled, collapsed in a heap and lay twitching.

The wand hissed again, retracting into its telescoping handle where it would remain coiled like an electrified version of Indiana Jones's bullwhip. Rox knew this because she knew the weapon, just as, without even looking, she knew the man who carried it.

Luke Freeman, hotshot CDC toxicologist…and the ex-lover who'd deserted her, sick and miserable, in a third-world hospital two years earlier, proving once and for all that "in sickness and in health" wasn't in his vocabulary when adventure called.

Damn him.

There was absolute, utter silence for a half second, broken only by the sound of the wind and rain. Then Luke muttered a curse and crouched down to touch her shoulder. "Rox? You okay?"

No, I'm not okay, she wanted to snap, because her body was still vibrating with electricity, along with another sort of heat, one that came from memory and hurt. Her stomach balled on a heave of denial and the small, childish wish that she could close her eyes and make all of this go away.

None of it was okay. It wasn't okay that people were dying in Raven's Cliff. It wasn't okay that turning down Aztec's casual dinner invite had nearly cost her her life. And it was seriously not okay that when the CDC finally got around to answering her call, they'd sent the one person she'd specifically requested they *not* send: Luke "I'll love you when it's convenient" Freeman.

Ignoring his helping hand, she pulled herself off the wet pavement and turned her back on him. She took her time swiping her hair out of her face, trying not to think about what she looked like—sopping wet with the stress and grief of the past seventy-two hours written on her face.

Then again, why should she care? Whatever they'd had between them had died years ago. She was a different woman than the one he'd known, smarter and stronger and far more aware of what mattered and what didn't in the long run.

Telling herself that their past relationship fell squarely into the "doesn't matter" category under the present circumstances, she gave up on her appearance and turned to face her ex.

He stood in the street, heedless of the rain, with three other people at his back. Silhouetted against the fog-diffused illumination from the streetlights above, he looked larger than life, like a hero come to the rescue.

And he'd probably practiced the pose, she thought sourly as she limped to close the distance between them, and took stock.

With short brown hair, glittering brown eyes, chiseled features and a mouth that was—as usual—tilted in a crooked grin, Luke looked good. Then again, he'd always held up under even the worst circumstances, so she'd expected him to look good. What she hadn't expected was the flare of memory that sucker punched her in the gut at the sight of him.

Her chest tightened and heat flashed through her, a complicated mix of heartache, anger and betrayal. She'd thought she was over him, that she'd gotten past wanting some sort of explanation for what he'd done. Now she realized she'd been lying to herself.

How could you leave me like that? she wanted to ask him.

Instead, she lifted her chin and said, "Thanks for the rescue. Then again, you always were good at making a grand entrance." Implying that his exits weren't nearly so slick.

His eyes went dark and his expression flattened, but he didn't rise to the barb. Instead he gestured to Aztec, who had gone limp with the aftereffects of the Taser zap. "I take it this is what you meant by 'some patients have been exhibiting violent tendencies' when you called the CDC?"

"Trust me, if I could've handled it on my own, I never would've put out the SOS." Her voice was sharp enough to have Luke's three teammates shifting and looking at each other behind his back.

There were two men and a woman. One of the men was a tall, lean guy with a pronounced right tilt to his aquiline nose, while the other was shorter and stockier, and wore a beard. The woman was dark-haired and pretty, and stood a little apart from the men. All three of them, along with Luke, were wearing jeans and sturdy boots, and blue hooded raincoats emblazoned with the CDC's sun-ray logo.

Luke crouched down beside Aztec without touching the fallen man. "Talk to me," he ordered Rox.

So much for introductions, she thought. She sent an apologetic glance toward the rest of the team, but they looked as if they were used to their leader's rudeness.

Then again, she remembered how that worked. You either figured out how to live with Luke's mannerisms or you hit the road. It wasn't like he was going to change.

"Roxie?" Luke prompted.

Gritting her teeth at the nickname, and the familiar peremptory tone she'd once found sexy, she ran through the typical symptoms of the Violents. They developed red-tinged eyes and yellowed skin, followed by fever and a profound shift of mental paradigm—as compared to the nonviolent patients, who typically presented with the same red eyes and yellow skin, but progressed to fever and malaise, followed by neurological symptoms such as loss of coordination and speech. In both cases, the patients became catatonic approximately six hours after the initial symptom onset, though some had gone down almost immediately, while one of the Violents had lasted nearly a day before collapsing, and had taken two innocent victims during that time.

She finished by saying, "Symptomatic treatments are maintaining the patients' conditions so far, but they're not showing any improvement, and my gut says they could crash at any moment. The two disease-related deaths were people I didn't get to in time."

And the guilt of that weighed heavily. She'd been too slow to recognize that what she'd initially thought was a low-grade flu epidemic was actually far worse. Because she'd been too slow to institute the house-to-house searches, there had been four deaths. Retired fisherman Elmer Tyson and his wife Missy, who had lived in a small cliff-side cottage north of town, had died holding hands in their shared bed. Michael Thicke, the chef recently hired to improve Raven's Cliff's single Italian restaurant, and his sous-chef, Brindle MacKay, had both died of stab wounds sustained when local boat mechanic Douglas Allen went Violent in the middle of his appetizer course.

All because of the disease, and Rox's too-slow reaction time.

When she finished her recitation, Luke nodded slowly, still staring at Aztec. "Is it infectious?"

"Not as far as I can tell, thank God," she answered. "There's no evidence of second-stage transmission." Meaning that she hadn't identified any cases where one victim had contracted the symptoms from another. "Unfortunately, that's about all I know. There just hasn't been time to go any deeper."

She told herself she shouldn't feel guilty, that she'd done the best she could. But deep down inside, small insecurities kept saying, *You know how to handle outbreaks. You should've been able to get the disease under control in the first day or so.* If she had, there wouldn't have been any need to call in reinforcements.

"No help from the locals?"

"The area hospitals aren't willing to risk having a patient go bad. They're just not set up for the level of restraint the Violents could need if they break out of catatonia."

"And you are?"

"I'm making do," she said firmly. "The Violents we've identified so far are restrained on cots in holding cells at the police station, and the cops are doing door-to-door sweeps twice a day, looking for the early symptoms. The chief of police has instituted a curfew, and Mayor Wells held an emergency town meeting this evening to let people blow off some steam."

Luke glanced up at her, brown eyes intent with the look she knew meant he was shuffling and filing every bit of information in the mental log he kept of each case. "You don't like the mayor." It wasn't a question.

Shoot, Rox thought. She'd been trying to keep her voice neutral. "You should probably form your own opinion."

"I trust your judgment."

The simple four-word statement probably shouldn't have annoyed her, but she found herself bristling, wanting to scratch at him for acting like he respected her opinions after he'd treated them like they meant nothing before.

But that was the key, she reminded herself. That was then. This was now. So she took a deep breath to settle the flare of anger, and said, "Wells is a little on the slick side for my taste, and rumor has it he's got his eyes on bigger and better, and doesn't mind making deals to get things done."

Luke shrugged. "Sounds like a politician to me."

"Yeah." Rox left it at that because she didn't have any real reason to dislike Mayor Wells. Just her gut feeling that his charming smile hid things that weren't in the best interest of Raven's Cliff or the town's inhabitants.

"This disease have a name?" Luke asked.

"The residents are calling it the Curse."

"Why?"

She lifted one shoulder. "Local legend about a fishing captain and a lighthouse—not important." She didn't think now was the time to get in to the town's recent problems, which had ranged from the loss of the mayor's daughter, Camille, in a freak wedding-day accident, to the discovery that they had a serial killer in their midst, one who thought he could lift the Captain's Curse by brainwashing women and sacrificing them to the sea.

Some said the bad luck had come with the arrival of the reclusive stranger who'd bought a property outside of town, some that it was attached to the destruction of the Beacon Lighthouse five years earlier...while others said that it dated as far back as the late 1700s.

As far as Rox was concerned, the superstitions were nothing more than a way for the locals to deal with a serious run of bad luck.

She didn't deal with luck, she dealt with science.

Luke frowned. "Since when do you discount legends? You were usually the first one looking to bring in the local medicine man and ask him to do his voodoo schtick and help heal the village from the inside out."

"That was Africa and this is Maine—it's a little different. Besides, this time *I'm* the local medicine man," she said, but her voice lacked bite as she felt the weight of the responsibility, and the failure. "And so far my 'schtick' hasn't made a dent, so I'd appreciate it if you and your team could get to work ASAP."

Luke looked at her for a long moment, expression

far more complex than the surface charm she remembered. Finally, he nodded. "You're the boss. That is, assuming you want us to stay."

He was giving her an out, an option of sending him away. Only there wasn't any possibility of that, because her people were dying and she couldn't help them on her own. *He's here and there isn't time to request another team before more people die,* she told herself. In the end that was what it came down to.

She'd come back to Raven's Cliff because she'd wanted a more personal relationship with her patients than the here-today-gone-tomorrow life of relief medicine. Now, the town needed her to set aside her past history with Luke and accept his expert help.

Telling herself that she could handle this, that forewarned was forearmed when it came to men like Luke Freeman, she turned to his three teammates, who were still ranged behind him as though waiting for the go-ahead.

Rox stuck out her hand. "I'm Dr. Roxanne Peterson. Welcome to Raven's Cliff."

FROM THE DARK SHADOWS beside Lucy Tucker's junk store, Tidal Treasures, the Seaside Strangler stood in the rain and watched the doctors carry Aztec's motionless form to the police station.

Part of him was disappointed that the others had arrived when they did. He'd been poised to come to Roxanne's rescue, ready for her to see him as a protector rather than just another part of the town's background scenery. Then again, it was probably best that he hadn't needed to expose himself like that. He had far more important work to do.

Secure in the knowledge that Roxanne was safe for the moment, he eased back along the junk store porch, knowing what he had to do next to ensure that she and all the other innocents in Raven's Cliff would be released from the threat that hung over the town.

He'd done it once before, and his sacrifice had bought the town peace for five long years. Then, just a few months ago the curse had come back and the gods of the sea had risen up and demanded another sacrifice. He'd tried to appease them once already, but he'd been thwarted, and the townspeople had rejoiced at the woman's safe return.

Just look what that got them, he thought in a flare of righteous indignation. *An epidemic. A disease straight from the halls of hell, one that turns men twisted and evil.*

As far as he was concerned, there was only one way to abate the curse and bring peace to the town of Raven's Cliff.

Another Sea Bride would have to be sacrificed.

Chapter Two

Within twenty minutes of Luke and the others carrying the groggy Violent into the Raven's Cliff Police Department, the briskly efficient officers on duty had gotten the patient secured in a cell and called in the chief of police and the mayor to meet with the CDC team.

After a round of introductions, Luke sent his teammates—clinical specialist May O'Malley, geneticist Bug Dufresne and biochemist Thom Harris—to check on the patients down in the holding cells and back at the clinic, and do something about Rox's busted-in door.

Then, as Rox started telling the mayor and chief of police about what the CDC team could do that she couldn't, Luke leaned back and watched them, dropping into detached-observer mode partly so he could avoid thinking about his own reaction to seeing Rox again, and partly because his job was often as much about local politics as it was medicine.

When he'd first left relief work for a coveted job as head of a CDC outbreak response team, he'd discovered that the protocol was pretty consistent whether he was covering an outbreak of hemorrhagic fever in Africa or a cluster of food poisoning from bad burgers in middle America. When he first showed up at an outbreak site, the powers that be always welcomed him with open arms, but as time passed, he invariably discovered local undercurrents that affected his ability to do his job.

As such, he made a point to figure out right away who was who among the players, and what they were likely to think about outside intervention.

In this case, he pegged Captain Patrick Swanson as a straight shooter who would help if asked and stay out of the way otherwise. The chief of police was a barrel-chested no-nonsense guy in his fifties, who came off as the epitome of a career cop who pretty much lived and breathed for his town. He was exactly the sort of guy Luke liked to have on his side.

Consistent with Rox's warning, Mayor Perry Wells was another story. He was probably the same age as Swanson, but that was where the similarity ended. Even though he'd been rousted out of bed near midnight, the mayor was neatly put together in casual slacks and a designer pullover, and didn't let his charm—or the perfectly calculated degree of tension on his face—slip for a second. Luke pegged him as a politician's politician, and figured he'd be one to watch.

"I trust Roxanne implicitly," the mayor said, turning to Luke. "If she says you're the best man for the job, then I know we're in good hands."

Luke suppressed a grim smile. He knew damn well she hadn't said anything of the sort—she'd called him "experienced" and "competent," a description that, although accurate, was probably better than she thought he deserved.

Swanson said nothing, just kept looking from Rox to Luke and back again, as though trying to figure out the source of the obvious tension humming in the air between them, evident in the way she didn't look at him unless she had to, and the distance that gapped between them in the wide lobby of the police station.

Luke was tempted to tell the police chief not to worry, that it was personal and wouldn't affect the job. That he'd been a complete bastard to Roxie, saying he loved her and then taking off without an explanation.

Granted, there'd been an explanation once, but its statute of limitations had long since expired. Besides, Luke figured it was better to let her hate him and move on with her life than try to make excuses that would only complicate things further. As a doctor, he knew the clean cut was almost always preferable to lingering pain. Unfortunately, he hadn't been able to keep it clean. The moment he'd gotten wind of her call to the CDC, he'd been on the phone mobilizing his team and pulling the strings necessary to get them assigned to Raven's Cliff despite her having specifically said she didn't want him.

She might not have wanted him, but from her brief description of the outbreak, he'd known she needed him, so he'd booked the flight and headed for north-coastal, middle-of-nowhere can't-get-theyah-from-heyah Maine.

He'd told himself it was because he owed her, and because he was the best in the business. But now, standing in the same room with her, all too aware of how her short, light brown hair brushed against her sun-kissed cheeks, and how her soft hazel eyes skimmed over him rather than latching on, he knew he'd made a fatal mistake in coming to Raven's Cliff.

If he'd really been thinking about her and about what he owed her, he would've stayed far away, because the moment she'd turned and looked at him out there in the rain, the moment their eyes had locked again after nearly two years apart, he was right back in that crazy, stirred-up place he'd been in the day he left her.

And damned if he didn't want to jump back in and make exactly the same mistakes again, even knowing the things that'd come between them two years earlier hadn't changed one iota. If anything, they'd gotten worse.

"What do you need from us?" Captain Swanson asked, unfolding from the cross-armed position he'd held as he leaned up against the front desk of the police station.

It took an almost physical effort for Luke to pull his attention away from Rox and focus on the case, warning him that he'd better get his head in the game, pronto.

"We're going to need a place to spread out," he said, thinking of the wide variety of scenes he and Rox had worked together before. "Someplace where we can safely restrain the violent patients, preferably with a couple of levels of security." He paused, then turned to Rox. "You know the sort of place we need. Any suggestions?"

There was a long pause before she said, "There's an abandoned monastery on the edge of town that'll suit. It's got several wings we can segregate, the rooms have sturdy, lockable doors and there's plenty of space for the lab equipment. The place is in the middle of the forest outside of town, and there's a high fence surrounding the entire property."

"Sounds perfect." And it did sound perfect, but he could hear the reluctance in her tone, warning him that it wasn't as simple as that. "What's the bad news?"

She grimaced. "Depending on who you listen to, either the people who've lived there over the years have all been overly imaginative, or the place is haunted." She lifted a shoulder in a half shrug. "Either way, it gives me the creeps."

Frankly, Luke was starting to think the whole town was creepy, from its pea-soup fog banks and the burned-out lighthouse he'd glimpsed from the road, to the haunted monastery and the sickness that turned normal people into monsters.

But he'd long ago learned that beneath differences in politics, religion and superstition, human beings all had the same basic biology. And that was what he had come to cure.

"The monastery it is," he said, not wanting to waste any more time discussing it...or thinking about the woman standing opposite him. "Let's get started."

The sooner he figured out what was going on in Raven's Cliff, the sooner he could fix it and get out of town before he did something really stupid...like try to pick up the pieces of a relationship he'd deliberately sabotaged two years earlier.

ROX TOOK HER OWN CAR to the monastery because she needed the space, and needed to know that she could leave at any time—assuming her patients didn't require her attention, of course. She hadn't ever—and wouldn't ever—put personal issues ahead of her patients' safety.

She had a feeling she might be tempted over the next few days, though. Somehow she'd forgotten how potent Luke could be in close quarters. Or maybe he'd grown even more so over the two years they'd been apart.

The Luke she remembered had been handsome and charismatic, a born leader who could make even the most resentful medicine man grateful for his help, and who could convince even the most insecure patients they were going to live. And he was still all of those things now…with the addition of a darker undercurrent she didn't remember, one that hinted of shadows and sadness and more complexity than he'd had before.

Worse, that dark sexiness only made him more compelling.

All of which meant she could be in some serious trouble, she thought as she drove the winding road leading to the monastery in the rainy darkness. Behind her was a convoy composed of the CDC team and a crew of a dozen off-duty cops, fishermen and other healthy locals Captain Swanson had talked into volunteering to get the monastery ready for patients.

Trees crowded close on either side of the road, bending down beneath the gusting wind, making her feel trapped in the dark tunnel of their branches. Or more accurately, it was the man in the black SUV directly behind her that made her feel trapped.

Why had Luke come?

If the fates had sent him as a test, she'd already

failed. She was supposed to be over him, damn it. Instead, she couldn't stop thinking about the look he'd sent her as they'd left the police station—part speculation, part heat, as though she wasn't the only one suddenly suffering sexual flashbacks.

Then again, why wouldn't he think of her that way? They'd been good together. Hell, they'd been better than good. The months they'd spent partnered through the Humanitarian Relief Foundation had been pretty much a blur of clinic hours and sex, both of which had been incredibly satisfying until their little differences had become bigger ones, and he'd taken the easy way out, leaving her with plenty of money to get home once she'd recovered from her fever, along with a breezy note about a dream job with the CDC. The note had contained nothing about them, nothing about the future he'd promised her.

"Which is exactly why I'm keeping my hands and all other body parts to myself this time," she said aloud as she pulled up to a pair of heavy wrought-iron gates set into a high brick wall. "Been there, done that, bought the heartache."

And if she told herself that a few million more times, she might even stop thinking about how wide his shoulders stretched beneath the CDC windbreaker. He'd gained a few pounds since she'd seen him last, and damn, they looked good on him.

"Stop it," she finally told herself. "There are far more important things to worry about right now."

Then again, the threat of the Violents and the deadly disease gripping her town was probably why she was fixating on Luke. Guy problems were normal. What was happening in Raven's Cliff was far from normal.

It was almost as though the town truly was suffering under an evil curse.

"So deal with the disease," she told herself, because that was the only thing she could hope to fix. "We work it one step at a time. First step—move in to the haunted monastery."

Trying not to talk herself into being even more creeped out than she already was, she got out of her car and used the keys Mayor Wells had given her to release a heavy padlock. The gate resisted at first, then gave way with a groan and swung inward. Aware of the others watching her from their idling cars, she blocked the gates open, climbed back in her car and drove along the narrow stone driveway leading to the monastery.

When her headlights picked out the main building, she saw that it was just as dark and creepy as she remembered, if not more so.

The stone building towered three stories high and stretched nearly the length of a football field on either side of the main entrance. The structure was made of heavy granite blocks, with marble pillars and peeling white-painted wood trim covered in a thick layer of moss and ivy. A series of narrow windows were nearly hidden beneath the dense greenery, glinting like the eyes of a predator peering through underbrush.

Built back in the town's heyday by the founding family, the Sterlings, the monastery had been a glorious place through the 1800s and early 1900s. Like the town itself, though, it had seen better days. Now the marble was cracked and crumbling, and the air blowing in through the vents of Rox's car carried the scent of decay.

"I wish I'd never mentioned this place," she said, trying to ignore the faint shiver working its way down the back of her neck. "We could've made do at the clinic."

Then again, that would've meant being in very close quarters with Luke. Maybe the monastery wasn't such a bad idea after all. At least she'd be able to put a few doors between them, giving her some space. Some privacy.

She avoided the road leading to the parking lot off to the side of the huge stone building, and instead pulled up right in front of the wide stone stairs leading to the main entrance.

All the better for a quick getaway if I need one, she thought wryly, but deep down inside she knew that even though the idea of escape might be sorely tempting, she wasn't going anywhere. This was her home. These were her people. If there was anything she could do to heal and protect them, then she'd do it, even if it meant spending the next few days—or longer—with Luke.

Speak of the devil, he was already out of his car and jogging up the main stairs, lighting the way with a heavy metal flashlight she knew from years past could double as both illumination and self-defense.

When she joined him, he flicked the cone of light in her direction. "No ghosts yet."

"I didn't say *I* thought it was haunted," she said. "But wait until you get a load of the interior. If there was ever a place that deserved its own horror flick, this is it. Around here it's a rite of passage for kids to sneak into the monastery and spend the night." It was also a prime make-out spot, but she didn't want to go there.

She tried a couple of keys, found the right one and got the front door unlocked. It opened with a theatrical creak that had a few of the volunteers shifting from foot to foot and looking at each other as if unsure this was such a good idea.

"Let's get the electricity on first," Luke ordered, taking charge of the situation. He gestured to one of his male teammates. "Thom, you can find the central panel, right? The mayor said we'd have juice if we hit the main breaker."

Thom, a tall, lean biochemist with a crooked nose, nodded and clicked on his own heavy flashlight. "I'm on it."

Within a few minutes, a scattering of lights came on, illuminating the entryway and glowing farther into the sprawling stone building.

Like the outside, the once grand inside of the stone monastery had fallen into disrepair, with splashes of graffiti painted on many of the walls, and the charred remains of a campfire sitting smack in the middle of the entranceway.

Luke looked around, his gaze lighting on the religious motifs carved into the lintels over each door, then picking out the three main archways leading from the entrance. He glanced at Rox and raised an eyebrow. "Suggestions?"

"Our best bet is to close off the east wing," she said, pointing to their right. "That's where the most vandalism has taken place, and according to local legend, it's also where things tend to go 'bump' in the night."

He nodded. "Not the best place to stick patients who are already mentally compromised. We do that and we're just asking for problems."

"Among other things." Rox pointed straight ahead. "We'll want to keep the kitchen wing open. Besides food, that'll be our best bet for setting up lab space. We can put the patient and sleeping rooms in the west wing." She jerked her thumb left, toward a locked door that had so far defied the vandals' efforts to break in. "I was in there on a field trip once, and I'm pretty sure I remember there being decent-looking rooms with sturdy doors. No doubt Captain Swanson can hook us up if we need to change out the locks or anything."

"This place is cool," Thom said, emerging from the shadows of the east wing and making them all jump slightly. He had a smudge of dust on the shoulder of his drying CDC raincoat, but his eyes were lit with an adventurer's curiosity that sent a faint pang through Rox. He continued, "Somebody should use it for a school or something."

"They tried," one of the off-duty cops said. "Since the seventies, it's been used as a boarding school, a summer camp for smart kids, a corporate retreat and a wellness center. None of them lasted long."

"That's 'cause it's haunted," one of the fishermen said. "We shouldn't be here."

There was a general mutter of agreement and more shifting of feet, but before Rox could jump in with her "now let's be rational" speech, Luke raised his voice and said, "I don't know much about ghosts. What I do know is that you have a medical emergency here, and it's my job to get it under control. So here's the plan. Thom, you take half of the volunteers and see what needs to be done to get the north wing functional as both a kitchen and a field lab." He gestured to his shorter, bearded teammate. "Bug here will take the rest of you into the west wing to get the rooms set up. Rox, I want you and May to head back to your clinic and prep the patients for transport. I'll stay here and troubleshoot. We'll have this place ready to go by dawn."

If anyone else had said something like that, Roxanne would've laughed, but she'd seen Luke create a workable triage and quarantine area out of even less, so she had no doubt he could transform a falling-down monastery to suit their needs in under five hours.

She nodded to May, a pretty brunette who had introduced herself as the team's clinical specialist. "We can take my car," Rox said. "You need anything from the SUV?"

May shook her head. "I'm good to go."

But before Rox could turn away, Luke called her back. "Wait." He held out a .22 she hadn't known he was carrying. "Take this. There could be more out there like your friend Aztec."

The memory brought a shiver, and she reached out to accept the small gun without protest. As she did so, her fingertips grazed his palm.

The touch brought a spear of unexpected, unwanted heat that had her drawing away from him, had her voice going husky when she said, "Thanks."

He nodded, eyes suddenly dark and hooded. "Be careful."

She left before she said—or did—something she'd regret, like ask him why he'd left her two years earlier, or why he'd come back to her now. They both knew there were other teams that could've taken the Raven's Cliff assignment.

The question was, why hadn't he let them?

"RUMOR HAS IT you've got the CDC on your doorstep," a mechanized voice said the moment Mayor Wells answered the ringing phone.

"Do you have any idea what time it is? And why the hell are you calling on this line?" Sitting on the edge of his king-size bed, Wells gripped the handset so hard the plastic creaked in protest. "Beatrice might've answered."

In reality, it would've taken far more than a ringing phone to disturb his wife. She'd been using tranquilizers heavily ever since the previous month, when their daughter Camille had fallen from the rocky cliffs into the sea during her wedding—her *wedding,* for God's sake.

Her body hadn't been recovered yet, and both the mayor and his wife were stuck in a state of seesawing hope: they hoped that her body would wash up so they could bury her properly, while praying she didn't, because as long as her body hadn't been found they could pretend she might still be alive.

Wells envied Beatrice the oblivion she'd found in the tranqs, but he didn't have the luxury of succumbing to grief because he had a town to run. Despite his best efforts, the whispers about the Captain's Curse had been growing louder over the past few months, even before the outbreak.

And now this.

"The doctors won't be an issue," he assured the man on the other end of the phone, who he knew only as a string of numbers from a Swiss bank account that made regular deposits into his own. "They won't be looking anywhere near your chemical purchases. You have my word on it."

The mayor was sweating lightly, though.

"Make sure they don't." The line went dead.

Wells sat for a minute, holding the handset to his ear, staring out the window into the black, rainy night. Then he stood and went to the wall safe where he kept an unregistered gun locked and loaded. He pulled out the weapon, checked the safety and tucked the firearm into the inner pocket of his briefcase.

Just in case.

Chapter Three

By midmorning, Luke's team and the volunteers had not only managed to clean and sanitize the kitchen and thirty small residential rooms in the west wing of the monastery, they'd also moved the patients from the clinic and police station into their new quarters.

The three Violents—Aztec Wheeler, boat mechanic Doug Allen and Jake Welstrom, a father of four whose symptoms had been identified during one of the house-to-house sweeps, thankfully before he hurt his family or himself—were locked in stone-walled rooms with barred windows, located at the back of the west wing.

The eight other patients—including Rox's clinic assistants, Jeff and Wendy Durby, as well as all four members of the Prentiss family plus librarian Cheryl Proctor and gas station attendant Henry Wylde—were housed in the middle of the west wing, in well-ventilated rooms under lighter precautions.

The doctors had staked out rooms close to the entryway, giving them equal access to the patient rooms and the kitchen, which would serve as both mess and lab. There, the members of the CDC team were working on processing the first set of blood and urine samples for analysis.

The outbreak response was up and running, and Rox knew she should be incredibly grateful. Instead, as she stood in the middle of the entryway watching the organized chaos that would hopefully put her town on the road to recovery, she felt a pang of resentment.

She'd barely been keeping ahead of the symptomatic treatments on her own, never mind being able to investigate the sickness or its cause, but there was a part of her that didn't want the others involved. She kept feeling as though she should've been able to handle this by herself, in her own clinic.

"Bug has the first set of blood samples spinning down," Luke said, appearing in the archway leading to the kitchen wing. "We should have some preliminary results in fifteen minutes or so, and that'll give us a starting point for figuring this thing out."

He'd changed out of the dust-smeared clothes he'd been wearing the last time she'd seen him, into jeans and one of the long-sleeved button-down shirts they'd both favored on assignment. Made of a high-tech nylon composite, the garments looked like cotton, but wicked away sweat and heat, and were nearly indestructible.

The sight of the shirt—and the fact that she'd long ago donated hers to Goodwill because she would never need them again—sent a little jab beneath Rox's heart.

Luke made a wide gesture to encompass the monastery, which was slightly less creepy in the light of day. "What do you think?"

"I think you made good on your promise to get this done by morning," she said, and her thoughts of a moment before made her voice sharper than she'd intended, lending accusation to the words.

"As opposed to other promises I didn't make good on, you mean?" Boots ringing on the stone floor, he moved to face her, expression resigned and maybe a bit impatient. "Go ahead. Ask me why I left you the way I did."

In other words, he was willing to talk about it if she wanted to fight. He might even be willing to say he was sorry for the way he'd left, though not for the actual act of leaving. But she could tell from his expression that it was going to be the same sort of circular argument they'd excelled at during the last few weeks before she got sick, the ones that never ended with a winner or a loser, just the incompatibility of two people who had great sex but wanted different things out of life.

She'd been looking to slow down and scale back to something more intimate at a time when his career had been poised to take off. Part of her had known the end was coming for them even before he'd left, but she had never expected—and could never forgive—how he'd abandoned her in a field hospital, sick and alone.

"I don't need to ask," she said calmly. "You left because the CDC put out an emergency call. Fine, I get that. But if you've got a guilty conscience because you weren't man enough to tell me goodbye to my face, you're just going to have to live with it. You earned it."

They locked eyes for a long moment. Finally, he nodded. "Fair enough."

"Fair enough," she echoed. In a deliberate effort to shift the subject back to where it belonged she said,

"Have you had a chance to check out my patient notes?"

He nodded, both to her question and, she suspected, to her change of topic. "They're pretty good, given the circumstances."

She didn't bother to defend her scribblings because she figured "pretty good" was an accurate assessment. By the time she'd figured out she had a major problem on her hands, the patients had been coming in so quickly and their symptoms had been so severe that she'd been hard-pressed to do more than scrawl a few details on each chart.

"I was thinking I'd talk to the families and get a better idea of what the patients have been exposed to lately," she said. "We still haven't seen any evidence that it's transmitting person-to-person so I'm betting on a toxin."

"Of course it's a toxin," he said, as if that should've been obvious. But his eyes lit with the same adventurer's interest she'd seen in Thom's expression the night before, the same kind she used to live for. "Question is, which one, and where is it coming from?"

When she felt that same adventurer's excitement stir sluggishly in her blood, she shoved it aside, telling herself that the mystery had mattered in a different lifetime, to a different woman. Not now, and not to the person she'd worked hard to become.

"I'll ask around town, get a victim profile and get back to you." She turned away, suddenly needing to get out of there, to get away from him and his teammates.

"Hey, Roxie?" he said, calling her back.

She turned, hoping he couldn't read her emotions the way he once had. "Yeah?"

"You still have the twenty-two?"

She patted the pocket of her light windbreaker. "Right here. I hate to admit it, but I feel safer carrying it, especially after what happened last night with Aztec."

"Good. You've got my number, right?"

She grimaced. "Don't count too heavily on cell phones. The coverage is pretty spotty out here, and there are dead zones like you can't believe."

"Then watch yourself, and be back by dark." He paused, and something moved in his expression. "You and I are on night shift together."

He turned and disappeared into the kitchen wing before she could ask whether that had been his idea or someone else's. She didn't call him back, though, because she was pretty sure she didn't want to know either way.

WHEN LUKE REACHED the utilitarian kitchen, he was relieved to find the large space deserted, save for a bank of portable auto-samplers doing their thing on the first set of patient blood samples. That gave him a moment alone to lean on the wide farmer's sink and look out the window, seeing nothing but Rox's face in his mind's eye.

He saw the terror on it when she'd run from the Violent. He saw the defiant expression she'd worn just now as she stood up to him. Even more, he saw the woman he'd known back then, and how her face had been so much more open, her laugh so much easier than it was now.

Back then, she'd said she wanted to slow down, to do something smaller and more intimate than the relief work they'd both loved. *I want to belong somewhere,* she'd said, as though belonging to him hadn't been enough.

Well, she was a part of Raven's Cliff now, and the way she'd interacted with the police chief and the volunteers—even the blowhard mayor—suggested that she belonged.

So why did he get the feeling she still wasn't happy?

"She's living in the middle of an outbreak site, you idiot," he said aloud.

These people were her responsibility, which made it personal for her in a way he'd never ever wanted to experience. But because it was personal for her, and dangerous for her, and hell, his damn job, he'd do his best to figure out what was making her people sick, and how to stop it. And then...

And then nothing. He'd leave, which was exactly what she wanted. She'd made it clear just now that she didn't need an explanation or an excuse from him, didn't need an apology. She wanted her town healed and him gone.

"I can do that." Ignoring a faint sense of disquiet, he strode to one of the auto-samplers and hit a few buttons harder than necessary, making the machine beep in protest.

"That's not going to get it to work any faster," Bug said from the outer kitchen doorway, which led to a small courtyard. "Science takes the time it takes."

"I know." Luke turned away from the machine to glare at the stocky, bearded geneticist. "And don't quote me to myself."

"Sorry. Just thought you might need a dose of rational detachment and good old scientific perspective." Bug crossed the flagstone kitchen to check how many minutes were remaining on the analytical program. Way too casually, he said, "You going to put me on bedpan duty for the rest of the year if I ask about her?"

Luke muttered a curse under his breath. He'd known his teammates would ask about him and Rox. He'd just been hoping it would be later rather than sooner.

The four members of the outbreak response team spent too much time in close quarters not to know each other well. May, their most intuitive member by far, had picked up on the vibes right away, and had asked him about it the night before. "Rox and I have a history," he'd answered, and hoped she'd tell the others what he'd said, and they would leave it at that.

Apparently not.

"Maybe not bedpans," Luke said, "but dishwashing at the very least."

Bug pretended to think about it. "I can live with that. So what's the deal? You two are giving off enough sparks to power a couple of sequencers and a cryofridge."

Luke would've winced, but he couldn't deny the observation. Things between him and Rox had never been subtle. Something that strong just couldn't be hidden. Unfortunately, it couldn't be controlled, either. Couldn't be trusted to last.

"She and I used to have a thing."

"No kidding."

"I ended it."

"And from the looks of it, not very well."

This time it was Luke's turn to say, "No kidding."

He didn't bother trying to explain. Rox didn't want to hear it, and it wasn't anyone else's business but theirs. So he said simply, "We're here to do the job, end of story."

Bug seemed to consider that for a moment before nodding. But as he turned away and busied himself removing small tubes from the centrifuge and placing them in a rack, he said, "If you want to talk about it sometime, you know, I wouldn't mind. I used to be married."

Luke couldn't tell if Bug thought that made him an expert on relationships or exes. "Used to be?"

"She wanted to stay home and do the family thing, and she didn't want to do it alone, so she found a guy who didn't disappear for weeks at a time on zero notice." The geneticist's shrug conveyed a sense of inevitability. "I don't blame her, and I don't blame the job. I love the job. The two just weren't compatible."

"Sorry to hear it." Sorry but not surprised. It was something of a theme in their line of work—the couples who made it were typically the ones who worked together, not the ones who struggled to keep things going long-distance. Then again, the couples who worked together also had a nasty habit of flaming out in public. It was a completely no-win situation as far as he could tell.

Just then, the auto-sampler beeped to announce that it had finished its first run. Relieved, Luke reached out and clapped Bug on the shoulder. "Let's see what we've got here."

He'd rather solve an unsolvable outbreak than try to figure out interpersonal relationships any day.

The two men peered at the computer screen, where

the results of the preliminary blood and urine tests were displayed.

"What the hell?" Bug recoiled in surprise, then leaned back in for a second look. "Their hormone levels are off the charts!"

And it wasn't just one or two of the levels that were elevated, Luke saw. The plasma levels of cortisol, aldosterone, testosterone, DHEA, estrogen and several others had spiked in every one of the sick people. More important, the levels were nearly double in Violents compared to the nonviolent patients.

"Not just any hormones," Luke said grimly. "Steroid hormones."

"The Violents are on a 'roid rage?" Bug said, surprised. But then he nodded. "It fits the symptoms, sort of."

"Doesn't account for the fever, the red-eye or the jaundice," Luke said, punching a few keys to bring up another data screen. "The white blood cell counts are within normal limits, so it's not an infection. Or at least not one the patients' bodies are recognizing yet and mounting an immune response against. Maybe something is attacking their thermoregulatory functions." Along with several other systems, he realized, as the skewed lab results continued to almost—but not quite—explain the symptoms.

"We're still missing something," Bug said, frowning at the results.

"Yeah. The trigger." Luke ordered the computer to print up the results. "Let's sit down with May and Thom and put our heads together. We need to go through all the environmental toxins and poisons, natural and unnatural substances that could have these

effects. Hell, maybe we're even looking at a mixture of agents, a pesticide or something. DDT messes with estrogen levels in pregnant women. Maybe our answer is something along those lines."

Bug paused at the doorway. "You want me to invite Roxanne to sit in?"

"Don't even try matchmaking," Luke said without rancor. "And no, leave her out of this. She's in town interviewing family members. With any luck, she'll come up with a common thread. If we can figure out the 'what' and she finds the 'how,' we should be able to nail this illness before anyone else dies."

And then he could get the hell out of Raven's Cliff.

"HOW MUCH LONGER will Henry be unconscious?" Mary Wylde asked. Jiggling a tow-headed toddler on one hip, the young mother looked exhausted. Her gas station attendant husband had been sick for nearly four days. Thankfully he wasn't among the Violents, but his vitals weren't good.

If he didn't turn around soon, Rox feared he might not recover. "I don't know how much longer," she said honestly, "but a team of specialists is working on him now."

"Oh." Mary's expression relaxed fractionally. "Thank God."

Rox had heard a version of that reaction from every family member she'd spoken to so far, and she was trying not to let it bother her. *Be grateful for the help,* she kept telling herself. *What matters most is saving lives and preventing new cases. Ego doesn't come into it.*

Still, she couldn't help feeling as though she'd failed

the town, and herself. She'd spent the past two years trying to make herself part of Raven's Cliff, yet many of the townspeople seemed to have more faith in the CDC outsiders than in her. Maybe it was because they remembered her fly-by-night father and his wild schemes. Maybe because some of them were still old-school enough to have more faith in a male doctor than a female.

Or maybe, in the end, it was because she just didn't belong anywhere in particular, no matter how hard she tried.

"Well, if there's nothing else…" Mary said, starting to ease back and shut the door as another baby began to wail inside.

"Wait." Rox held up a hand. "I just have a couple of quick questions." She ran Mary through the survey she'd come up with, mostly focusing on the patient's habits and how they differed from those of the family members who hadn't gotten sick.

Mary answered the questions as quickly as she could, casting glances back in the direction of the escalating cries. She pointedly didn't invite Rox inside so they could continue their conversation, but that was okay. The young mother's answers only confirmed what Rox had begun to suspect three houses ago.

She was pretty sure the Curse had something to do with locally caught fish.

The day before the symptoms began, three of the victims had eaten fish and chips prepared at the Cove Café. Two others, including Mary's husband, had eaten fish purchased at Coastal Fish, a seafood market located adjacent to the piers. Mary, on the other hand, had eaten a salad because she was trying to lose ten pounds before beach season.

Rox's gut told her she had the beginnings of a pattern. Maybe she should've seen it sooner, but seafood was a staple of the local diet, and the symptoms were nothing like typical food poisoning. It hadn't been until she had the time to really compare her patients' diets that the obvious answer had jumped out at her.

Okay, so I've got a pattern, she thought as she headed away from Mary's house, jotting notes as she walked. *Now what?*

She had several other people to interview, but she was less than a block away from Coastal Fish. Instinct told her she should keep following up with the families, but her gut told her she already had her answer, and what could be a better next step than going directly to the source?

Knowing that working with a team meant being part of the team, and liking the feeling of connectedness, even if it came with Luke and their shared baggage, she pulled out her cell phone, intending to call and let him know what she'd discovered. But when she flipped open the unit, she saw the searching icon displayed.

No signal.

"Damn it." She looked around, halfway thinking she'd head to her clinic and call from there, but the clinic phone was still down from the night before—it looked like Aztec had ripped the cable out of the exterior wall before he'd knocked on her clinic door…which was scary enough that she was trying not to think about it.

Besides, Rox thought, the reception was even worse out by the monastery, so Luke's phone probably wasn't receiving, either. Odds were it would be a wasted effort.

Deciding that her best bet was to obtain samples of the various catches before driving back to the monastery, she headed for Coastal Fish.

The shop front was the epitome of New England kitsch, decorated with netting, weather-beaten buoys, lobster traps and plastic lobsters. When she pushed through the swinging door, she found the air inside cool and faintly moist, carrying the good scent of fresh seafood. With racks of sauces and bread crumbs on two walls and the third dominated by a huge glass display case, the place was unpretentious but did a brisk business because the prices were good and the fish came straight off the boats, which literally docked at the back door of the shop.

The owner of Coastal Fish, Marvin Smith, stood behind the counter wearing a crisp white apron and a smile that didn't quite reach his eyes. In his mid-sixties, stick-thin and balding, Smith had been the mainstay of the fishing community for many years until he'd retired to run the fish store. He was still the fishermen's unofficial spokesman when things needed doing around town, which was both good news and bad for Rox.

The good news was that if the fishermen had noticed anything strange lately, he'd know. The bad news was that she wasn't sure he'd tell her, because he'd find anything that threatened local fishing to be a personal threat, as well.

She checked, but saw no red tinge to his irises as

she stepped up to the counter, where a glass display case offered a wide selection of local favorites arranged on fresh greens, with plastic lemons strategically placed for a hint of color.

"I hear you brought in some medical detectives from out of town," Smith said in a gravelly voice. "Couldn't take care of a few fevers on your own? Business is off, you know. Much more of this and word's going to get around. It's the start of summer—we can't afford to lose the tourists."

"We're talking about far more than a few fevers here," she said, stung. "People are dying."

"Then why aren't you off running tests or something?"

I am, she thought, but knew she would have to tread lightly if she wanted to get anything out of the combative ex-fisherman. "We've split up to pursue various angles of the investigation. I'm collecting samples from the main food sources in town." She gestured to the door behind him, which led to a long, narrow room where the fish were filleted and weighed out. "Can I get back there? It won't take long."

"What won't take long?" It took a second for Smith to process her intention. When he got it, he narrowed his eyes. "You want to take my fish?"

"I just need a small sample of each type," she assured him, though she fully intended to take samples from multiple fish of each variety. The fact that the disease hadn't struck everyone who'd eaten fish over the past bunch of days suggested the source might be a certain type of fish, or maybe even one specimen that had yielded multiple cuts, or had gone through a certain processing machine.

"You going to pay for it?"

"Of course," she said, though it irked her to do so. A call to the police chief or the mayor probably would've cleared her way, but she preferred to handle things on her own. Besides, Mayor Wells had plenty to cope with right now—besides the outbreak, he was dealing with a vociferous group of locals who, at the town meeting the night before, had started pushing him to let local businessman Theodore Fisher buy and refurbish the burned-out Beacon Lighthouse, which some residents believed was the seat of all the bad luck Raven's Cliff had suffered in recent months.

Rox didn't put much stock in curses, but if rebuilding the lighthouse gave the town a common goal she didn't see why it was such a bad idea. The mayor, however, was doing his damnedest to block the project for some reason.

"Okay," Smith finally said, reluctance etched in his body language as he flipped up the pass-through and let her come behind the counter, then led her through the door to the processing area. "I guess I can't stop you from buying fish, can I?"

"Thanks." She moved among the big ice chests, trying not to make it obvious that she was checking each thermostat, each coolant line, looking for malfunctioning equipment that might be associated with the illness. "Do you supply the Cove Café?" she asked, trying to keep her voice casual.

"Why?"

"Just curious. I had an amazing cod sandwich there the other day and I was wondering if they purchased their fish through you." That wasn't entirely a lie— she'd had a good fish sandwich at the café, but it'd been more like a month ago, and she hadn't particularly cared where the fillet had come from. She was looking for an easy connection among the sick people.

He shook his head. "Nope. They buy straight off the boats."

Okay, so there went that theory. "You buy off the boats too, though, right? Have they been bringing in anything special lately?"

"Special in what way?" he asked, continuing to answer most of her questions with questions of his own, a technique she suspected was designed to put her on the defensive.

It was working, too. She found herself growing more tense as she worked her way into the processing room, toward where the narrow space opened directly onto one of the fishing piers. Smith followed close behind her, making her feel as though she was being stalked.

Or herded.

She turned to him. "Can you get me twenty or so of those little bags you use for small shellfish orders? I need to keep each of the samples separate. A grease pencil would be good, too."

He didn't budge, instead moving closer. His voice dropped to a growl. "What, exactly, are you going to test for?"

"That's up to the CDC team," she said, playing dumb.

"Where else have you taken samples?"

She was almost positive he would call and check, so she didn't lie. "You're the first."

Catching movement out of her peripheral vision, she turned her head and saw two men enter from the pier. One was moving strangely, shuffling his feet as though he was having neurological problems.

Panic knotted Rox's gut and her heart hammered in her ears. "Maybe I should come back later."

"I don't think so." Smith blocked her exit on one side, and raised his voice to call, "Hey, boys, the lady doctor here seems to think our fish is poisoning the town. What do you think about that?"

There was an ugly mutter from the men, and they moved to stand shoulder-to-shoulder, blocking her on that side as well.

She was trapped.

Chapter Four

Rox's heart hammered as the two fishermen approached and Smith remained unmoving at her back, blocking her escape.

She held her hands away from her sides, palms up. No harm, no foul. "Come on, guys, I'm not looking to start any trouble here. I'm just trying to do my job."

"By ruining ours," the big guy on the left said. "It's bad enough you're telling people it'd be good for them to eat tinned foods and drink bottled water, and you've got the coast guard telling us we can't put the boats into harbor anywhere but here. Now you're trying to prove it's the fish making people sick? What do you think's going to happen to the town if the feds shut down the fishing grounds? We'll starve!"

As he drew closer, she identified the dark-haired, dark-eyed man as Phil Jenks, a deckhand on one of the more prosperous fishing boats. He was big and brawny, shading toward overweight, and wore a plaid shirt beneath his waterproof coveralls. She'd seen him around town, didn't know anything good or bad about him, but he gave her a seriously not-good vibe as he approached.

"I don't want to ruin anything," she said quickly. "Don't you want to know if there's something wrong with the fish you've been catching? Better yet, don't you want me to prove that they're fine?"

She didn't mention that, based on her suspicions, there was a good chance they'd have to declare a moratorium on the fishing grounds until they had a chance to prove or disprove her theory.

Next to Jenks was Alex Gibson, a tall, sinewy guy with broad shoulders, brown hair and bright blue eyes. He was dating Lucy Tucker, the owner of the Tidal Treasures junk store located diagonally across from the clinic. Rox had chatted with Alex on occasion, and knew he was a fair-minded, mild-mannered guy who seemed to truly care about the town, and its inhabitants.

She leaned on that now, her voice rising a little with nerves. "Tell these guys, Alex. I'm only trying to help."

"Roxanne is okay," Alex said obligingly. "She's not the sort to start trouble."

"How can you be sure?" Smith muttered from behind her. "It's not like she's one of us. She's only been here a year or so, and that father of hers was a real piece of work—here today, gone tomorrow, and took a few of us for more than we could afford, without much to show for it."

It wasn't the first time she'd heard something along those lines about her salesman father, who'd promised far more than he ever delivered—it was more like the thousandth time she'd heard it, and she knew for sure it wouldn't be the last. Still, it stung. One of the main reasons she'd chosen to set up her clinic in Raven's Cliff was that it'd been one of the few places she'd lived as a child where she'd felt like even a little part of the community. As the town's only doctor, she wanted to become a larger part, the sort of person people turned to when they needed help.

She didn't want to be the enemy.

"I'm only trying to help," she said again. "Please. Let me test the fish. If I don't, there's a good chance the team from the CDC will want to, and that'll make it a federal issue, maybe even involving the Fish and Game Department, and we wouldn't want that, would we?"

Okay, that was bending the truth a little—the samples would be analyzed by the CDC team regardless of who actually took them, and once they had their answers, nothing she could do would stop Fish and Game from getting involved. But she didn't think now was a good time to mention that, as the men got close enough that she could see the whites of their eyes.

Alex looked fine. Jenks, though…she wasn't sure. His eyes might be a little bit reddish, and he definitely seemed to shuffle when he walked.

Her gut told her he was infected, and headed for a rage.

She backed away from Jenks, until she was almost touching Marvin Smith.

"Mr. Smith," she said quietly, hoping Jenks wouldn't hear, or if he did, that he wouldn't compute. "Jenks is infected, and I think there's a good chance he is, or soon will be, a Violent. I'm going to start backing up and I want you to do the same. I need you to pretend that we're going to talk in your office."

There was a moment of startled silence, as though

he was trying to decide if she was lying. Then she felt a touch on her elbow, felt Smith move up close behind her. Loudly, he said, "Let's take this into my office. We'll have more privacy there." He pushed her around in front of him. "Get moving, you."

He practically shoved her ahead of him, blurting, *"Run!"* Then he turned and flung himself at Jenks, shouting, "Alex, get out of here!"

And all hell broke loose.

Rox pulled Luke's .22, hit the safety and waited for her shot. Jenks was grappling with Smith, tearing at the older man's clothing and howling with rage, his vocabulary and speech devolving as his eyes turned redder by the second. Definitely a Violent.

"Marvin, get out of the way!" Rox yelled. "I've got a gun."

Alex took off running, headed out the back way, shouting over his shoulder, "I'll get Captain Swanson. Keep him here until I get back!"

"Hurry!" she urged him, heart pounding in her chest, palms sweating like they always did when she picked up a weapon with the intention of using it.

Finally, Smith was able to tear away from Jenks. Thinking fast, the retired fisherman rolled beneath the bolted-down sorting trays in the middle of the narrow shed, out of Jenks's reach.

Roaring, the sick, enraged fisherman turned on Rox. There was no mistaking the hatred in his red-tinged eyes, the urge to kill. "Got a gun, eh?" He sneered, grabbing a fisherman's gaff off the wall and holding the sharply pointed, reverse-hooked spear like a weapon. "You're a doctor. There's no way you'll shoot me."

"Run, Doc!" Smith shouted.

I just have to hold him until the cops get here, Rox thought, stomach twisting with fear, with the effort it was taking to stay more or less calm. *Just long enough to—*

Jenks lunged toward her, swinging the gaff in a deadly arc.

Rox screamed and ducked under the attack. The gaff slammed into the side of the sorting shed and stuck, and Jenks roared and yanked at it.

Taking a deep breath, Rox said, "I'm sorry, Mr. Jenks."

She shot him point-blank in the meaty part of his outer thigh.

Jenks bellowed and went down, clapping his hands to his thigh, where blood quickly stained his heavy pants.

"Just stay still and keep the pressure on," she said. "The police will be here in a moment. They'll help us. You'll be—" *Fine,* she was going to say, but didn't get the chance, because Jenks, heedless of the pain, scrambled to his feet and came at her again.

He took her by surprise and got her before she knew what had hit her. His hard, hot body slammed into her, driving her back against a sorting tray. Pain flared in her lower back, and when she struggled upright, she was forced to hunch over.

She realized she'd lost the gun the same moment Jenks figured it out, and dismay slashed through her alongside fear.

"I've got it!" Smith yelled. "Get out of here!"

Rox didn't stop to think or argue. She turned and ran, limping.

Three shots rang out behind her in quick succession, but a garbled curse and dragging footsteps warned that Jenks wasn't down, wasn't giving up on his pursuit. And he was moving faster than she was.

She put her head down and ran faster, adrenaline helping banish the sting in her lower back. Her breath whistled in her lungs as she skidded into the front room of the fish shop and through the passageway between the counter and wall, then across the store and onto the street, praying that the cops would be there, waiting to save her.

The avenue was deserted, even though it was the middle of the day. The terrified townspeople were hunkered down in their houses, waiting for Rox and the others to make it safe again.

Instead, she was running for her life.

Practically sobbing with fear, she bolted up the street toward the police station. Behind her, she heard Jenks's dragging footsteps, and then a terribly familiar click.

The .22. He'd gotten it away from Smith.

"No!" Rox threw herself off to the side as Jenks fired. The sharp report echoed along the deserted street. Another. Another.

Screaming, Rox zigzagged, trying to get him to use up his ammunition. How many bullets had been in the gun when Luke gave it to her? She hadn't checked, and damned herself for the oversight. She didn't know if the Violent was out of ammo or just waiting, didn't know where the cops were or why they hadn't yet responded.

Thinking fast, legs rubbery with fear and exertion,

she turned down the next side street, headed for the town common and the RCPD. If the cops weren't coming to her in time, she'd get to them.

Hopefully.

Refusing to consider the alternative, Rox pushed herself, running as fast as she could. Her lungs hurt; her heart hurt. What if she didn't make it? What if—

Motion blurred in her peripheral vision and a heavy body slammed into her. Strong arms grabbed her and dragged her to the side, into the narrow alley between the Cove Café and the library. Rox screamed and thrashed, but her attacker held on tight, keeping her in the alley and clapping a hand across her mouth.

"Roxie!" Her attacker shook her. "It's me. Knock it off, it's me."

It took a second for Luke's voice to penetrate, another for her to stop fighting and sag in his arms.

He wasn't another attacker. He was a rescuer.

Beyond the mouth of the alley, she saw Swanson and his men close ranks on Jenks, wrestling him to the ground as he kicked and screamed imprecations.

Shaking, Rox turned away from the sight and pressed her face into the nearest available solid, immovable object. Which happened to be Luke's chest.

"I thought I was going to die," she said, not caring that her voice trembled. "I thought he was going to—"

"Don't think about it," he interrupted, wrapping his arms around her more securely, and holding on tight. "You're safe. I've got you. Don't think about the what-ifs."

She wanted to lean into his embrace, wanted to inhale his musky, masculine scent, close her eyes and remember what it'd been like to be with him, to be his.

But she knew she didn't dare lean once because she'd be tempted to keep leaning, and that wouldn't work.

This was what he was good at—the heroic rescue. It was the day-to-day stuff he couldn't deal with.

Don't think about it, he'd said, and the familiar phrase echoed back to too many arguments, too many disappointments.

Luke liked things simple and surface. He didn't like to think about bad things—either the ones that had happened, or the ones that hadn't. When things got too intense, he pulled up stakes and moved on to the next town, the next village, the next assignment. Just like her father had.

And that wasn't what she wanted. Never had been.

As Rox's adrenaline leveled off, she told herself she didn't need to cling, not when there wasn't a single good thing that could come of it.

She pushed away, levering her arms between them and backing up before she looked at him. "You're right. I'm fine, so there's no reason to think of what might've been. I'm grateful for the rescue. Grateful to all of you." Deliberately turning away from Luke, she cast her eyes toward the cluster of cops at the mouth of the alley. She picked out the figure of an anxious-looking Alex Gibson.

When their eyes met, he raised a hand and called, "I'm sorry it took so long for me to get the police."

"You did great," she said, and meant it. "Thank you, Alex."

Still deliberately ignoring Luke—more because she was mad at herself for wanting to fall back into old patterns than because she was mad at him for being himself—she marched back toward the group clustered around Jenks. When Captain Swanson looked up, she said, "Thanks for the rescue, Patrick. Once you've got him secure you can take him to the clinic and I'll see to his leg."

Coming up behind her, Luke insisted, "He goes straight to the monastery."

"No offense, but I've got a better setup for minor surgery at the clinic," she countered without looking at him. "Once I've dealt with the leg wound, he can go to the monastery." Now she did turn and fix him with a look. "Unless you have objections?"

A muscle at his jaw knotted in a rhythmical tic, but he nodded once, sharply. "Fine. We'll do it your way." But his tone made it clear that it was only because he didn't have a real reason to object.

Otherwise, it would've been his way, all the way. As usual.

"Fine," she echoed, damning herself for responding to the tension in the air, for caring whether or not he approved of her decisions. And even worse, for caring that he hadn't once said he'd been worried about her.

LUKE KNEW HE SHOULD head back to the monastery and ride herd on his team. Instead, he found himself in the waiting room of Rox's clinic, kicking his heels while she patched up the Violent she'd winged with his .22.

The longer he waited, the worse his mood got.

He couldn't fathom what she'd been thinking, going into the fish shop by herself. She should've known better, damn it. It was one thing to do a basic medical history on the victims. It was another to walk into a man's space and imply that the product his liveli-

hood—and that of much of the town—depended on
might be contaminated.

She should've called in and waited for one of the
CDC team members to make it into town to provide
backup. Better yet, she should've finished her canvass
and brought her suspicions to the team, so they could
make some decisions, and a plan.

Instead, she'd gone completely Lone Ranger and
nearly gotten herself killed during the investigation.

The more he thought about it, the angrier he got,
which meant he'd built up a pretty serious temper by
the time the cops escorted Jenks out of the exam room.
The fisherman was shackled, stitched, limping and
disoriented, looking pretty close to crashing into the
catatonic state of the other patients. But that didn't stop
him from raging as the cops dragged him through the
waiting room and out the busted clinic door.

"You'll get yours, bitch!" he howled, his head
thrown back and his eyes rolling wildly as he craned
around, trying to see if Roxie had followed, if she was
listening. "This isn't finished. You don't come into
my town and threaten our fishing. No freaking way.
I'm going to get free, and I'll be coming for you!"
Head still tipped back, he let loose with a laugh that
started down low in his chest and rose up, and up, and
up, until it cracked on a near-shriek that riffled the
hairs on the back of Luke's neck.

"Let's get him out of here!" one of the cops shouted,
urging his buddies out the broken door.

Even once they were gone, though, Luke could hear
Jenks outside, sometimes laughing, sometimes shriek-
ing, gibbering meaningless strings of words that all
ended in threats against Roxie and her clinic.

"Cripes." Luke rolled his shoulders, trying to loosen the sudden tension. "Friendly town. Not exactly the sort of place I'd have rushed back to."

"Then again," Roxie said from behind him, "I bet you've never rushed *back* to anyplace. It's always the next stop with you, isn't it? The next village, the next outbreak, the next victim."

Luke halfway expected her to say "the next woman," but she didn't. He'd bet a year's pay she'd thought it, though, which brought his temper up another notch as he turned to face her, only to have it notch even higher when he saw the shadow of a bruise on her cheek, and the utter exhaustion in her eyes.

She looked defeated. Vulnerable. And very alone, standing in the hallway of her one-man clinic in the middle of nowhere.

Holding iron control over the anger, he said tightly, "We've had this fight before. Since we're not together anymore, I can't see that it's relevant."

It wasn't what he wanted to say, but it was better this way. He had to keep it clean, keep it simple. They'd tried the other way before and it hadn't worked for either of them.

"You're right," she said after a moment, shaking her head. "I guess I should apologize."

"Don't," he said with a kink of dark humor. "You'll just have to take it back when you've heard what I came here to say."

"You want me to leave," she said matter-of-factly. "You're going to point out that I've been personally attacked twice in less than twenty-four hours, and that most of the townspeople frankly don't like me. They consider me as much of an outsider as you, only worse, because I'm trying to pretend I'm a local. Then you'll probably offer to call in more CDC manpower, but only if I agree to stay away for the duration of the outbreak, until the great Luke Freeman has worked his magic, solved the mystery and saved the day. Then you'll leave and I can come home, and everything will go back to normal." She lifted her chin, as though daring him to disagree. "How am I doing so far?"

"You're right about everything except the towns-people. I hadn't realized you were that unpopular. I just figured it was the disease making the victims mean." And how revealing that her lack of popularity was the thing that seemed to gall her the most, he thought.

Then again, she'd always cared too much about other people's opinions, had always spent far too much of her valuable time befriending the locals, time he'd thought would be better spent working on science and medicine.

She shrugged and looked past him, to where the cops had stuffed Jenks into a patrol car and were doing a U-turn, headed for the monastery. "You're not a local until you've been here a dozen or so generations. And my father wasn't exactly—" She broke off. "Never mind. Not important."

"Your father what?" he asked, unable to help himself even though he knew they should keep it to business.

For all that she'd talked about wanting a home and family, she'd almost never spoken of her own, except to say that her parents were divorced, and her mother had remarried and moved to the Dakotas.

"Like I said, it's not important. What *is* important is that—as you've probably guessed—I have no intention of leaving Raven's Cliff. Not now, and not in the future. I'm staying in this town, and I'm staying on this case—period, end of sentence. So rather than waste time arguing about it, why don't you bring me up to speed on where your team is with the outbreak?"

He damn well *did* want to argue. He also wanted to grab her and shake some sense into her, or maybe grab her, stick her in the SUV and drive her right out of town, so he could lock her somewhere safe.

She narrowed her eyes. "Don't even think about it."

"I hate it when you do that," he muttered, piling annoyance atop the anger.

"I can read you like you're closed-captioned. Deal with it."

Except she hadn't always read him right, he remembered. She'd missed a few things along the way, and he hadn't bothered to correct her misapprehensions.

But that was then, not now, and now was what mattered. The outbreak was what mattered.

"Treat me like I'm the local medicine man," she said softly. "Give me that much respect, at least."

He snorted. "Please. My respect for your skills as a doctor have never been a question and you damn well know it."

"So stop treating me like an outsider!"

It was the second time she'd used the word, which made it telling. He didn't remember that being an issue before. Then again, those had been different times, different circumstances.

And they had, perhaps, been slightly different people.

He nodded. "Okay, medicine man. You're on." He gave her a quick summary of the tests they'd run so far, and the results, most of which had been negative except for the abnormal levels of steroid hormones.

"They're 'roid raging?" she said, her voice cracking with incredulity. "From a disease? That doesn't make any sense. I've never heard of anything like that before."

"Me, either, but that doesn't mean it's not happening now. God knows we've seen some pretty strange stuff before. Why not this?"

"You're right." She scrubbed both hands across her face, wincing when she hit the bruise. "I know you're right. And I know it's stupid to say 'but we're in Maine.' But we are, and that's the way I feel. This sort of thing shouldn't happen stateside, in my town."

He didn't point out that by her own admission most of the townspeople didn't consider it "her" town, nor did he remind her that bad stuff happened in the affluent U.S.A., not just the third-world countries they used to frequent. She knew both those things, she just didn't want to face them.

Denial was part of the grief process. He'd seen it before in hundreds of village doctors, priests and medicine men—healers all, who took it upon themselves to care for the people nearest them. Unlike Luke himself, who wasn't looking to care about anybody, and made no secret of the fact, to himself or anyone else. He was just looking to check off another outbreak and move on, because that was what he did. He moved on, and didn't get involved. It was better that way.

Reminding himself of that hard-learned lesson, he forced the anger—and the worry—aside. Roxie was a grown-up and a hell of a doctor. If she said she was staying, then she was staying. And that was a good thing, too, he told himself, because he could use the extra set of capable hands if he was going to solve the case.

That was the most important thing. Not the people, but the case. And he'd do well to remember it.

"We're wasting time standing here talking," he said curtly, crouching down to grab the field kit he'd snagged from the SUV. "Come on."

She looked surprised, though he wasn't sure if that was because of the abrupt subject change, or the fact that he was including her in the investigation. "Where are we going?"

"Coastal Fish. We have some samples to take."

THE WELL-DRESSED MAN cursed when a rock shifted beneath him, making him teeter on the narrow trail. With a sheer rock wall on one side and a deadly drop to the ocean on the other, he didn't have much room for maneuvering, and the full knapsack he had slung over one shoulder was messing with his balance.

Swearing bitterly, he scrabbled for a handhold and lunged a couple of steps farther forward, until he reached the place where the path widened to a small ledge.

From all other directions—at the top of the cliff, where Beacon Manor and its burned-out lighthouse looked out over the sea, or from the water looking up—the ledge looked like nothing special. But that was a natural optical illusion created by a fallen rock slab. In reality, the faint path and narrow rocky shelf led to a series of interconnected caves that delved into the cliffside below the lighthouse, above the waterline.

He entered the first cave, which was a wide, welcoming space with a scorched black spot near the entrance providing mute evidence of long-ago camp-fires. Moving quickly through this antechamber, he ducked a little to keep from banging his head and strode deeper into the cave system, lighting the way with a small flashlight that he retrieved from the heavy knapsack.

In times past, the caves had no doubt served as bolt-holes for smugglers and bootleggers, as suggested by the tool marks in some of the rock walls, and the smears of vintage graffiti in tar paint and scratched symbols.

Farther back, in the last chamber that was easily accessible by a full-grown man, a set of four iron eyebolts sunk into the living rock indicated that some-thing—or someone—had been locked there for a time.

Now, it served a similar purpose.

Before entering the chamber, he pulled a stocking cap over his face. It was a cliché, perhaps, and prob-ably unnecessary since his captive spent most of her time unconscious, and was completely out of it when he did manage to rouse her. But he figured the precau-tion was a sensible one given that his plans involved returning his captive to her home.

Assuming, of course, that her father played his part correctly.

The young woman was in her late twenties, and wrapped in a pale blue blanket that he'd tucked around the chains. Her tawny hair was a tangled mess of cork-screw curls plastered around her face, and her arms, legs and face were bruised and scraped, and streaked with dirt.

She didn't move when he entered, but the regular rise and fall of her chest assured him that she was still alive, still as out of it as she'd been ever since he'd handed over the fake documents to the distant hospital's staff, claiming their Jane Doe as his own.

He did his business with brisk efficiency, rousing her enough to force her to drink two cans of a liquid diet for senior citizens, followed by a bottle of water. Then he cleaned her up, wrinkling his nose at the smell and the mess, wishing there were another way to handle the necessary business.

But, he reminded himself as he packed the trash away in his knapsack and headed out of the cave system, *the reward is going to be well worth the effort.*

Either her father cooperated…or she died.

Chapter Five

Five hours and a number of lab tests later, Rox and the other doctors had an important new piece of data: yes, the outbreak was coming from the fish.

Specifically, they'd linked the symptoms to a group of abnormally large fish marked with a dark stripe along either side of their bodies. Mostly haddock and cod seemed to have been affected, though Rox suspected someone—probably Marvin Smith—had either hidden or dumped other examples of the abnormally large fish, because when she and Luke had returned to Coastal Fish to collect their samples, the bins had seemed much emptier than they'd been earlier in the day.

Regardless, their exhaustive analyses revealed that the blood and muscle of the dark-lined fish contained a substance very similar to an enzyme normally produced by the human body in order to increase steroid hormone production. There seemed to be two forms of enzyme contamination, with some fish producing a great deal of it while others produced more moderate levels.

"That explains the two types of the disease," Luke

said later that evening. "The nonviolent patients must've ingested the lower-producing fish, while the Violents ate the turbocharged version, *et voilà!*" He gestured with his fork. "The enzyme moves from the digestive tract to the circulation, triggers overproduction of steroid hormones and probably some secondary metabolites and products we haven't caught yet, and you've got yourself a 'roid rage."

Except, as far as Rox was concerned, there was no *et voilà* about it. There were still too many facets of the disease going unexplained. "That would be a neat little explanation," she said tartly, "except for one thing."

He simply raised an eyebrow.

"The Violents aren't randomly raging. What we're seeing is an amplification of their natural tendencies. Aztec's little crush on me turned into an obsession. Jenks's normal loyalty toward the fishing fleet became homicidal protectiveness. That's not random. It seems to me like it's more of a…" She thought for a second. "Like a loss of inhibitions."

The five doctors sat around the long table in the kitchen, discussing their findings over dinner. Bug had whipped up an army's worth of burgers and fried veggies, and Rox was enjoying the solid meal. She was having trouble remembering the last time she'd actually sat down and eaten.

Probably just before the first cases came in, she admitted to herself. She'd been on the go ever since. She should be grateful to Luke and the others that the patients were mostly stable and receiving supportive treatment in a safe environment, and she had time to sit down for dinner. But she wasn't grateful. She was feeling snappish and combative. It irked her that Luke had been the one to identify the enzyme, that Bug had actually been the first to notice that the larger fish all had the dark lines while their smaller counterparts didn't.

She'd wanted to be the one to discover the source and identity of the disease, wanted to be the hero who saved the town.

And she needed to get over herself, she acknowledged inwardly, knowing that her mood stemmed from the fact that while they might've identified the fish as the common denominator among the patients, they didn't know why the fish were growing so quickly and whether the problem was going to spread...and they didn't know how to treat the catatonic patients, some of whom were starting to deteriorate.

"Roxie," Luke snapped, his tone suggesting he'd said her name several times already.

"What? Oh, sorry." She blinked, realizing that she'd tuned out midconversation with her burger halfway to her mouth.

May, who was sitting next to her at the long, picnic-style table, touched her arm. "When was the last time you slept?"

"Last night," Rox answered around a jaw-cracking yawn that suggested her body had been waiting for her to notice how tired she'd gotten.

"We got here last night, remember?" Luke said. "First we took care of your buddy, Aztec, and then we went to work getting the monastery ready for business. Correct me if I'm wrong, but you were right there with us, all night."

"Which means you've all been up for going on two

days, too," she countered, not wanting him to single her out for coddling. Anything his team could handle, she could handle, too.

"True enough." Luke nodded. "But how many days were you doing three-hour night checks on your patients before that?"

She hated that he was being reasonable, hated that he was in her space, hated that he didn't seem to be experiencing any of the same flashes she was, when she'd see him tilt his head and grin a certain way and remember that same look from before, remember the situation and the people they'd been with, and how it had felt to be by his side. It hurt her that he seemed to be able to work beside her without thinking about the past, when she couldn't do anything but.

And, she admitted with brutal honesty, he was right, damn it. She was overtired, and getting bitchy. She sighed and scrubbed both hands across her face. "You're right. I'm cranky and exhausted and I'm no good to anyone."

May squeezed her arm. "You're not alone anymore, Doc. Turn it off for a few hours while someone else does night shift."

Remembering their earlier conversation, Rox glanced at Luke. "Weren't we supposed to be on night shift?"

"That was assuming you caught some downtime this afternoon. You didn't, so you're off the hook. Go on." He waved her toward the west wing. "Let someone else take care of you for a change."

She shot him a sharp look at that statement, thinking it was an odd thing for him to think, and an even odder thing to say in front of his teammates. But she didn't call him on it, and nodded instead. "Thanks. Wake me if you need me."

He nodded. "Of course." But they both knew he wouldn't. As far as he was concerned, the great Luke Freeman didn't need anyone—at least not for long.

Yawning, she rose and headed for the room she'd staked out as her own—which had consisted of dumping a suitcase full of toiletries, a few changes of clothes and other odds and ends she'd collected from her apartment over the clinic.

Her room was much like every other residential room in the monastery: a long, narrow stone rectangle with a door at one end and a single barred window at the other, with a cold stone floor and high ceiling. This particular room had a strangely carved pillar set in one corner. Only a handful of the rooms she'd been in had the pillars, which were no doubt some sort of structural element put in to support the huge weight of the monastery itself.

The volunteers had schlepped in borrowed cots for the doctors, along with bedclothes and the like, creating a bare but functional space. And at the moment, functional was all she was asking for.

Too tired to unpack and organize, she scrabbled through the contents of her suitcase until she found her toothbrush and toothpaste, and swept the rest onto the stone floor beside the bed. The shared bathroom was down the hall, which meant she had to pass several of the nonviolent patients' rooms. She looked in on Jeff and Wendy as she passed, hoping against hope that the married couple, both registered nurses who worked for and with her at the clinic, would start to show improvement soon.

There didn't seem to be any change in their conditions, which was both good and bad news—good because at least they weren't back-sliding like some of the others, but bad because the longer the human body stayed in a catatonic state, the less likely it was to recover.

They needed to find a cure soon, or a treatment at the very least. Granted, Luke and his team had made enormous progress in only a day, but it was hard not to feel as if they were playing catch-up to the disease, always one step behind.

Telling herself the dragging depression was as much fatigue as hopelessness, Rox used the bathroom and headed back to her room, locking the door from the inside. She knew the gesture was totally unnecessary, given that the Violents were catatonic, restrained and locked in their rooms, and Luke's teammates were on night duty, but it made her feel safer knowing she could sleep without thinking of Aztec and Jenks only a few doors down.

After taking a last look around her sleeping area— a habit from the old days when there had been snakes and various vermin to worry about—she flipped the light switch, killing the single bulb that illuminated the chamber.

She felt her way to the cot, tripping over her suitcase in the process, but she was too tired to care that she'd made an even bigger mess with her packed clothes. She got her shoes off and set them beside the flashlight she was keeping close by, in case the power went. Then the old familiar field training kicked in and she dropped onto the cot fully clothed, so she could respond quickly to a medical emergency or other sort of threat.

She thought it was a sad state of affairs that although she was in Raven's Cliff, less than five miles from her clinic, a threat or emergency wasn't out of the question. But she didn't think that for long, because she was asleep almost immediately.

She didn't know how long she slept, or what she dreamed of, but when she awoke, her breath was locked in her throat and her heart was hammering as though she'd sprinted all the way to Beacon Lighthouse and back. At first she thought she'd been dreaming.

Then she heard a shifting, sliding noise and she knew it was no dream.

Someone was in her room.

For a half second she thought maybe it was Luke, but that part of their relationship was long over. And she'd locked the door.

Sudden panic welled, and her pulse hammered so fast she could barely hear the sounds the intruder was making over in the corner farthest from the door. Moving slowly, she reached down to where she'd left her shoes, and felt for the flashlight.

Once she had the light, she raised it and aimed it toward the corner, where the shifting, scraping noise had become a low growling sound. Almost like a moan.

Bracing herself, Rox held her breath and turned on the flashlight.

LUKE AND BUG were on night shift. Having already done their first set of rounds, they'd hunkered down in the hallway, arguing over the best way to go about curing the poor townspeople who'd already come down with what they were calling Dark Line Disease—or DLD for short.

"We can't just universally block the steroid receptors," Luke said, running the possible scenarios in his head. "That'll mess with everything, not just the hormones being up-regulated by the DLD."

"So we'll have to target the enzyme that's coming from the fish," Bug said, nodding his agreement. "What if—"

He broke off as the muffled sound of a woman's scream came from Rox's room.

Luke was on his feet in an instant, adrenaline buzzing with the sudden kick of his pulse. "Roxie!"

He bolted for her closed bedroom door with Bug on his heels, and cursed bitterly when he found it locked from the inside. Damn thing was way too heavy to kick in, too. Pounding on the panel, he shouted, "Roxie? Unlock the door."

There was no sound from the other side of the thick wooden panel.

"Go get Thom," Luke said urgently. "There's a blowtorch in the SUV, and a crowbar. I want you to—"

He broke off when the lock clunked open with a heavy-throated rattling sound. The door to Roxie's room groaned open and there she was, standing fully clothed in the doorway without a scratch on her, clutching a flashlight in bloodless fingers.

Her face was deathly pale, her eyes dark holes in her head, as she stepped out into the hallway and very deliberately shut the door at her back.

She didn't throw herself into his arms, but she did look scared out of her wits.

"Nightmare?" Luke said, pulse leveling off a little once he saw that she was unhurt. "Rat?"

She shook her head. "No. I think...I think I just saw one of the monastery's ghosts."

Luke snorted. "No, really. Was it a rat?"

She glared at him. "No, really. I'm pretty sure it was a ghost. Or else—" She broke off, and some color returned to her cheeks, staining the skin with a blush. "Or else this monastery isn't as straightforward as it looks. Rumor has it there are secret passageways all through this place. Maybe someone was playing a joke."

But she wasn't laughing. Nor was she backing down from her insistence that she'd seen something...and Rox had never been one for hysterics or seeing things that weren't there. If she said she'd seen something, he was willing to believe her.

Question was, what had she seen?

He took the flashlight and opened the door. "Let's take a look." He glanced at her. "You want to go wait in the kitchen or something?"

She shook her head. "No. I want to know I'm not losing it."

"Then stay behind me," Luke ordered. "Just in case."

He stepped inside and flipped on the lights and saw...nothing out of the ordinary. The room looked just like the one he was staying in—a rectangular cell decorated in Early Solitary Confinement, with the addition of a carved pillar in the corner. Rox's belongings were strewn across the room, but he knew her well enough to realize that was standard Rox, not an interrupted search.

Thom and May joined Bug in the doorway, having been called from the field lab by the commotion.

"Everything okay?" Thom asked.

"Fine now," Luke said shortly. "You don't have to stay."

Thom lifted a shoulder. "Machines are doing their thing. I've got a few minutes."

Rox flushed, but said, "I was asleep, and something woke me—a scratching, shuffling noise, maybe a few clicks. I got the flashlight, thinking it was a rat, like Luke guessed. But it was something…" She faltered, but soldiered on. "It was human, there's no doubt about that. But it looked like it'd been dead for days, and was in an advanced state of decomp, with flesh hanging off it, gray-green skin, stringy hair." She shuddered. "If it was a mask, it was a good one."

Based on her story and the lack of evidence supporting an intruder, Luke was rapidly rethinking his belief that she'd seen anything at all, because the whole flesh-hanging-zombie thing sure sounded like a stress-induced nightmare to him. Most likely, she'd heard a tree branch scratching the room's single window and seen the shadow of her own foot, amplified by the flashlight beam.

When he'd first heard her scream, he could only think that one of the Violents had gotten loose and gone after her. But this was… This was just weird, and not at all like the Roxie he'd known. Which made him wonder what else about her had changed.

"So, say it was a mask," he began. "What would be the point? And, not to be picky on the details, but where did this zombie creature go after you screamed?

Your door was locked from the inside and the window's got bars across it."

She was already across the room, poking at the carved pillar and the wall on either side of it. "Come on. Help me look for a mechanism or something. There's a secret passage here, there must be."

But the pillar was just a pillar, and there was no sign of a pressure pad, no seam in the stone that looked as if it could be a doorway.

The longer they looked, the more sheepish Roxie got, until she finally called a halt to the search. Blushing, she said, "I'm sorry, guys. Luke must've been right in the first place. It was just a garden-variety nightmare bogeyman."

"Don't worry about it." Bug gripped her shoulder. "You've dealt with two real-life bogeymen since the last time you slept. I don't blame your brain for cooking up a scary dream or two."

She smiled. "Thanks." Her smile fell away when she looked at Luke. "Sorry to bother you guys."

The others filed out, but he stayed behind, not quite ready to leave her alone yet. He couldn't get past the terror on her face when she'd opened the door, or his own quick panic when he'd realized she was locked inside and he couldn't get to her. "You want to switch to a room without a pillar?" he asked.

She started to refuse, but then said, "You know, I think I will. Is there a spare room set up?"

"Take mine," he said automatically.

"I don't think that's such a good idea."

"I'm not suggesting we share." He lifted a shoulder. "I'll grab what I need for tonight. You take my bunk, I'll take yours, and tomorrow we can swap out our suitcases and stuff."

And if there was a small chest-beating part of him that just flat-out wanted her sleeping in his bed after her scare, she didn't need to know about it.

She nodded. "Okay. Thanks."

"And don't lock the door this time."

He waited while she collected a few things from the mess strewn across the small chamber. Typical Roxie, he thought with an inner grin. Her treatment area, first-aid kit and field notes were always hyperorganized and meticulously complete. Her personal space, not so much.

Once she was out the door, he took a long last look around, trying to see something her half-asleep brain would've turned into a flesh-hanging-zombie creature, but nothing jumped out at him. Shrugging, he stepped out into the hallway, closing the door at his back.

Thom, May and Bug were waiting for him, expressions grim. Roxie stood nearby, and she'd gone ghost-white again.

"Boss," Thom said. "We've got a problem."

Luke's pulse quickened. "What happened?"

"It turns out Rox's nightmare wasn't a nightmare at all. It was a distraction intended to get us all in one place."

A very bad feeling took root in Luke's gut. "What happened?"

"Someone trashed the field lab."

TRASHED WAS THE operative word, Rox realized the moment the four of them stepped into the enormous kitchen. The food prep machines at one end of the big room were untouched. The field lab, though, was a disaster area, with machines tipped over and liberally streaked with spray paint and white foam, with parts scattered across the floor.

"They cut the power cords and took them," Thom reported, voice hoarse with anger. "The laptops are gone, the sequencer is full of what looks like Silly String, and the little punks filled the injection ports of the gas chromatograph with shaving cream."

"Kids," Rox said, ashamed that she'd bought into their ploy and screamed like a baby when she saw the "ghost," and even more ashamed that it was kids from her town that'd done the damage. "It has to have been some of the high schoolers—they're up in arms because Captain Swanson has been talking about canceling the prom later this week. They must've broken curfew and gone looking for trouble."

"They found it," Luke said tightly. "Call Swanson. I want the cops to check houses and find out which kids aren't where they're supposed to be."

Rox nodded and went to find her cell phone. She had just enough signal to make the call. "He's on his way," she reported, returning to the kitchen a few minutes later. "He said not to touch anything. They'll want to take pictures and document the damage."

Luke, who had his own cell pressed to his ear, nodded in her direction. "Thanks." Moments later, he raised his voice and snapped, "I don't care where the equipment is supposed to be going and how much Donegal thinks he needs it. I want it here tomorrow by noon at the absolute latest, understand?" Apparently the target of his wrath got the idea, because he nodded. "Good. Make sure it does."

Snapping the phone shut, he said, "We'll have replacement machines here in the morning."

You could've tried saying "please" and "thank you" before biting the poor person's head off, Rox thought. But she didn't bother saying anything of the sort because that was another "been there done that" fight between the two of them.

She cared about feelings, he cared about results.

"Bug and I will meet with Swanson," Luke said. "Thom and May, you're off-duty, so get some cot time. Roxie, I want you to tell the cops what you saw, and then try to get some more sleep. Tomorrow's going to be a long day."

"Like today was short and sweet?" But she nodded. "I'll take you up on a few more hours of z's."

But it was nearly two hours later before Swanson and his men had arrived, gone over the scene and taken her statement. They gave her room—or the room that had been hers, anyway—a thorough going-over, but couldn't find any trigger mechanism or evidence of a hidden door.

There had to be one, though. She hadn't imagined what she'd seen. The vandalism was proof of that.

Wasn't it?

By the time the cops left, dawn was staining the horizon salmon-pink and she was wide-awake. Knowing there was no way she was getting back to sleep at that point, she elected herself to do morning rounds.

After sticking her head into May's room to let the clinician know she was off the hook for the 6:00 a.m. shift, Rox pulled on a white coat over yesterday's clothes and donned latex gloves and a mask.

Granted, she hadn't used the precautions earlier during the outbreak and had remained healthy, but now there was a reverse risk that she would transmit a secondary infection to the patients who'd been sick the longest.

The last set of tests had indicated their white blood cell counts were plummeting, suggesting that they were becoming immuno-suppressed. If their bodies lost the ability to fight off other diseases, they could die from something as simple as a cold while Rox and the CDC team raced to find a cure for the DLD.

Suitably protected, she made the rounds, starting with the nonviolent patients. Jeff and Wendy were still holding their own, as were the others, with the exception of the youngest member of the Prentiss family, four-year-old Tony Prentiss, whose white count was continuing to fall. Worse, he was starting to develop fluid in his lungs.

They needed a treatment soon, or more people were going to die.

Thankfully, Captain Swanson had acted on their information and enacted a temporary ban on fish sales in and from Raven's Cliff, and suggested that surrounding towns do the same. He'd also ordered the local fishermen to catch and kill as many of the overlarge fish as they could find, and preserve the bodies for scientific examination. Samples from the DLD fish and human patients were on their way to the main CDC lab, as well as several area veterinary schools and the Fish and Game Department, on the theory that the more scientists they had working on the problem, the better.

All of that meant there shouldn't be any new cases, and there was some hope that they'd have a treatment in hand sooner than later, God willing. But as Rox continued her rounds, she couldn't get past the feeling that they'd only seen the tip of the problem, and that there was worse yet to come.

Maybe it was the vandalism and the knowledge that someone outside the team and the patients had been in the monastery with them, or maybe it was just the eerie quiet of the halls, but she almost felt as though someone was watching her as she moved from room to room, checking vitals and changing IV bags as needed.

"Don't be silly," she said aloud, trying to talk herself out of the creep-factor. "You're imagining things."

She got through the nonviolent patients without incident, but when it came time to do the other end of the hallway, she stalled.

Call her a wimp, but she didn't want to go in those rooms alone. Aztec and Jenks were catatonic and restrained, but each of them had tried to hurt her. Intellectually, she knew she'd be safe, but still, the idea of being in close quarters with either of them—not to mention Doug Allen, who'd killed two people, and Jake Welstrom, who might've done something equally terrible if the cops hadn't found him just as his symptoms became apparent…

Rox let out a long breath. "Don't be a wuss. You can do this."

But just as she was dredging up the courage to unlock the first of the doors, she heard Luke call, "Wait up, I'm here."

The hail was followed by the sound of his footsteps as he came around the corner from the main entryway. Wearing bush pants and one of his indestructible field shirts, with his short brown hair casually tousled, he looked incredible.

She would've resented that he looked that good when she was feeling achy, overtired and frumpy...except she was too glad to see him just then to resent anything.

He ducked into the supply room, where they'd organized their protective equipment and basic supplies, and quickly pulled on a white coat, gloves and a face mask. When he rejoined her, he said only, "Ready to tag-team the Violents?"

She nodded. "Thanks."

"Don't mention it."

And as she moved to unlock Aztec's room, she realized he actually meant it. He wasn't looking for applause, wasn't trying to be a hero. He'd noticed she was doing rounds and hadn't wanted her doing the Violents alone, and he'd quietly stepped up to help her out.

The Luke she'd known before would've made a big production out of it, would've made sure everyone knew what a great guy he was.

As they set to work, she said, "You've changed."

She halfway expected him to brush off the comment, or make light of it. Instead, he stopped what he was doing and crossed the room, ushering her out into the hallway, away from the patient, and then moving to stand very close to her.

His body heat warmed her even through her clothing and protective equipment, and she caught her breath, thinking he'd taken her comment as an invitation and was unsure how she'd react if he made a move. On one hand, she knew all the reasons she should stay away from him.

On the other, though, the attraction was undeniable, and if he'd changed, if he'd grown out of his wanderlust ways...

Almost as though he'd caught her wistful thought, his voice went very low, very serious, when he said, "Maybe I've changed some in little ways, yeah. But I'm the same guy, Roxie, make no mistake about that."

She shivered a little, fighting a strong sensual pull that was part memories of the man he'd been, part attraction to the man he'd become. "I don't know what that means."

He eased closer and pulled down his mask, then did the same for hers. "I'm the same guy—the guy you ate with, slept with, worked with…." He leaned closer still, until his breath feathered on her suddenly sensitized lips as he said, "I'm the man you made love with, the man who loved you as best he could."

He hesitated for a second, their lips a whisper apart. Either one of them could've closed that gap and made the promise of a kiss into a reality.

But then he eased back a fraction and said, "But I'm also the guy who can't stay in one place for longer than a few weeks without it being time to move on. I'm a grandstander and a fly-by-night and all the things you ever called me. None of that's changed." He paused, and his eyes went dark with a passion she felt in her own core. "If you want a reprise for old time's sake, just let me know. The chemistry's still there, and sex was never our problem. But don't go telling yourself that I've evolved, or that things will be different this time, because I can promise you they won't be. I'm still the same guy."

Rox blew out a breath. "Well. That was blunt." She wasn't sure how she felt. She was disappointed, yes. But also maybe a little relieved, in an odd way, to have it out in the open between them.

The corners of his mouth tipped up. "One of the few things you never called me was a liar."

"That's true." Or it had been, she realized, until the day he'd left her. He'd told her he loved her, and as far as she was concerned, that included an implied promise not to abandon her in a foreign hospital, sick and alone.

That memory should've been enough to have her backing away right then and there. But she'd been alone for too long in Raven's Cliff, even before the outbreak. And she was so cold now, from the chill of the stone monastery, and from the sense of watching eyes. So rather than doing the smart thing and backing away, she took a step forward.

"Roxie," he said, his voice low in warning. "Be sure before you start something you'll regret later."

"I'm not starting anything," she said, and knew it was the truth. "I'm finishing it. Call it closure, call it once more for old time's sake… Call it whatever you want. I'm going to call it the goodbye kiss I never got."

Working methodically when her hands wanted to shake and her pulse wanted to race, not even entirely sure what had gotten into her, she stripped off her gloves. Then she got him by one lab coat lapel in each hand and used that purchase to rise up onto her toes as his eyes went dark and her own blood heated.

He moved as she did, and they met halfway.

And kissed goodbye.

Chapter Six

About two seconds into the kiss, when it went from lips to tongues, Rox's rational side started sending out serious warning signals.

What are you doing? What were you thinking? Stop this now before it's too late!

The thing was, it was already too late, because before any more time had passed, the voice of reason lost out to the pounding of her pulse and the race of heated blood through her veins.

Luke's taste was achingly familiar, yet brought with it a sharpness she didn't remember, an edge of sensual energy that speared straight to her core and left her wet and wanting in a heartbeat.

When she'd first stepped into him, he'd brought his hands reflexively to her hips. Now, as the kiss deepened, he began caressing her—long, slow strokes that started at her nape and cruised down across her hips and back up again. Smooth strokes. Tantalizing caresses.

Murmuring pleasure, she crowded close, pressing her breasts against him, molding herself against his muscular form. She slid her hands from his lab coat lapels to his shoulders, then around to the back of his neck, where his short hair was soft and sleek.

One kiss flowed into the next, and then another, each more blatantly sexual than the last until they were plastered together, twined around each other. They were as close as two people could be while clothed and standing, and it still wasn't close enough for Rox, who started thinking about the bedrooms down the hall—

And that was so not a good idea, she realized, a dash of cold reality cutting through the sensual haze.

She didn't pull away, but she must've stiffened in his arms or made some small sound of dismay, because his kiss went from hot, hard and demanding to a soft touch. An easing away.

They broke apart by unspoken consent and just stood there, leaning against each other. Rox's pulse hammered in her ears and she was breathing hard, but so was he...and no wonder. Like he'd said, sex had never been the problem between them. It was other stuff that got in the way—like their complete lack of common goals.

Which was why she'd kissed him to say goodbye.

Right.

"Okay," she said after a moment. "That got a little out of hand."

She felt a chuckle vibrate through him. "I'm not complaining."

She should've been grateful he was willing to let it go. Instead, anger spiked that he hadn't been as affected by the kiss as she'd been, that he could brush it off so easily and turn it into a joke. She pushed away from him with a glare. "And that would be one of our irreconcilable differences. You don't take anything but your career seriously."

The old Luke would've laughed that off. The man he'd become, the one she didn't know nearly as well as she kept thinking she did, leaned in, his expression darkening. "Let's get one thing straight here. I took our relationship very seriously. I was never unfaithful, and I never told you something that wasn't true. You were the one who changed the rules on me and got mad when I wouldn't go along with the new program."

"That 'program'—" she sketched the word with finger-quotes for emphasis as her anger built to match his "—was exactly what I said I wanted from the beginning. It's not my fault you thought I was kidding when I said I wanted to be a small-town doctor, have a little house of my own, a husband, a family…all those traditional and *permanent*—" she emphasized the word, knowing that was the hang-up front and center "—things you can't stand."

He stepped away, holding up both hands as though showing her that he was unarmed, or maybe calling for a time-out. "And there we have it. The last four weeks of our relationship condensed into a sound bite. Thanks so much for the memories."

She lifted her chin. "And thanks for the goodbye kiss. Let's hear it for closure."

They stood and glared at each other for a few seconds before he muttered a curse and turned away. He bent down and scooped up the surgical gloves they'd both dumped during the kiss. "Let's get fresh gloves and masks. Then we can finish rounds."

"Of course," Rox said. They were, first and foremost, doctors there to do a job.

Luke headed into the storeroom to get new masks. Just as he was coming back out, a new set of footsteps sounded in the hallway. At first Rox was grateful, thinking she could pass off rounds onto one of the other clinicians and get a little breather from the scene she and Luke had just had. But then she heard a drag to the footsteps, a faint unevenness.

"Luke," she said softly. "I think we have a problem."

Moments later, May came around the corner, ashen-faced and nearly staggering. When she saw Luke, she said, "Hey, boss, I don't feel so hot."

"You don't look so hot," he agreed, stepping forward and taking her arm, keeping it casual even as he paled and his voice went rough with concern. "Let's get you someplace where you can lie down."

He met Rox's eyes over May's head, and she saw an anguish that matched her own.

May's eyes were shot with red, her skin sallow.

They hadn't stopped the spread of the disease, after all.

OVER THE NEXT five minutes, Luke went through the motions, but he was seriously reeling from the one-two punch of shocks to his system. Punch one—kissing Rox—had his blood running hot and his brain crowding tight with warm fuzzy memories he'd long ago told himself to forget. Then had come punch two—May getting sick.

That brought back memories, too—but they weren't good ones.

He helped Rox and Thom set May up in her bedroom, helped them start the palliative treatment immediately, hoping like hell it would be early enough—or just plain *enough*—to keep her from sink-ing into the same coma the other patients had dropped into. But even as his body moved through the familiar medical procedures by rote, he was cringing inside.

When May lay back on her pillow, her dark hair fanned away from her too-pale face, he saw another face. When Thom set the IV in her arm, he saw another's arm, another set of IV bags drip-drip-dripping clear fluid that might or might not prolong life.

Rox sent him a look. "Luke, are you feeling okay? You look off."

Thom didn't bother checking his boss. "He doesn't do so well when people he knows are sick. A stranger dying of hemorrhagic fever? He's the man. But put a teammate in the bed and he's a mess. I remember this one time—"

"That," Luke interrupted grimly, "is more than enough."

"No," Rox countered. She got a sudden determined look on her face, and he could practically see the pieces starting to come together in her head. "Really, it's not. But rather than get Thom in trouble by pressing him, I'll ask you directly. Is that why you checked out on me two years ago? Because I was *sick?*"

Part of him wanted to lie and say that yeah, that was exactly what'd happened. Because if she thought that, maybe she'd forgive him, and maybe they could try again with the kiss they'd just shared. Maybe it could go further. Maybe they could go back there, for old times' sake. But he knew her well enough to know that it wouldn't be any "old time's sake" on her part— whether she admitted it or not, she'd be looking for the gold at the end of the rainbow, the white picket fence and two-point-five kids, and all that stuff that was on his mental medic alert bracelet under the category of "fatal allergies."

And while he might have played a few games in his time, he'd never promised more than he could deliver. Like he'd said to her before, he didn't lie. He didn't always tell the whole truth, granted, but what he did say was truthful.

So he shook his head. "I'd love to pretend it was, Rox. I'd love to say I bailed on you because I looked at you in that bed and panicked, thinking you were going to die and realizing how much you meant to me. But the honest truth is that I knew you were on the mend, I got the e-mail from the CDC, and I figured it was a graceful way to end something that was already on the rocks."

The Roxie he'd known before—particularly the volatile person she'd become in the last few weeks before she'd gotten sick—would've handed him his butt on a platter for that one. He was expecting to get raked, hoping for it almost, as a way to relieve the tension that'd sprung up hard and hot between them after that so-called goodbye kiss.

But instead of flaring, the woman she'd grown into merely nodded. "Well, that's honest. Insulting and tactless, but honest."

She finished May's chart and set it near the bed. Then she glanced at her watch. "My caffeine headache says it's time for a cup of tea. You guys want anything?"

Luke declined. Thom nodded. "Coffee'd be good." When she was gone, he turned and gave Luke a serious "what the hell?" look. "I can't believe you said that."

Shrugging to relieve the tension in his shoulders,

Luke turned and looked out the barred window at the overgrown grounds of the monastery, so he didn't have to look at May, who had fallen asleep while they were talking. "It was the truth. At the end, Rox and I were clawing at each other more than we were getting along."

Or rather, he'd been clawing and she'd been too quiet. She'd already made her decision. He'd been the one fighting for something that no longer existed.

"Yeah, but, dude. That was harsh."

"Better than letting her think I've evolved or some such garbage." But even as he said it, a hollow ache gathered in his chest, because there was a small part of him that wished he could say exactly that.

Which just went to prove that he wasn't the slightest bit evolved—he'd even lie to himself if it increased his chances of getting laid.

Feeling a faint burn of shame that he'd reduced things between him and Rox to that basic level, he waved to Thom. "Come on, let's finish up in here and get Bug. We need to put our heads together and figure out how May got sick when she hasn't eaten any local fish, and—"

He broke off as a sudden terrible thought occurred. He was out the door like a shot, shouting, "Roxie, don't drink anything!"

He found her in the kitchen with two steaming cups sitting on the counter and her eyes saucer-wide. "You're right," she said before he'd even said anything. "The vandalism might've been a distraction on top of a diversion. Whoever did the damage might not have been just trying to slow us down. They might've been trying to stop us permanently."

Thom, who'd come in on Luke's heels, said, "You two are finishing each other's sentences. One of you want to explain?"

Luke turned to him, heart still hammering in reaction to his sudden fear that Rox might've ingested something from the monastery kitchen. Which she hadn't, thank God. He said, "What if, hypothetically, those too-large fish were created on purpose?"

"Why would someone want to do that?"

Luke grimaced because Thom was right. They were getting into serious conspiracy theory territory here. "Work with me, okay? Let's say for whatever reason, those fish were contaminated on purpose. And let's say whoever did the contaminating doesn't want it figured out or stopped. If he—or she—thought we were getting too close to figuring things out…" He trailed off and raised an eyebrow.

Thom nodded. "He—or she—might break in and spike our supplies with the contaminant, figuring on disabling one or two of us, maybe more, and confusing the investigation by making it look like it was an infectious agent rather than a toxin." But he didn't sound convinced. "Seems like a long shot, boss. More likely it's a rapidly mutating virus or something, so we're seeing multiple versions in the same outbreak, some that're violent, some that're nonviolent, some that're infectious…." He trailed off. Shrugged. "You get the picture."

"Yeah," Luke agreed. "And I can't argue the logic, either."

"But you still want to rule out the contaminant theory, right?" Thom guessed.

"Yeah," Luke said again, too aware of Roxie, and

how she was still staring at the mugs, as though they might jump at her or something. "Rox? You okay?"

"I drink tea when I'm in the clinic, Jeff and Wendy drink coffee. And I don't know if they had any fish. What if..." She shook her head. "No. It doesn't play. It doesn't make any sense for it to be something like that. This is a small town, a tight-knit community. Everyone likes everyone else. This isn't the sort of place where stuff like you're suggesting happens."

He decided not to call her on the "everyone likes everyone else" theory when he knew damn well after only a couple of days that the statement was patently untrue. He'd chatted enough with the cops who'd helped set up the field hospital to know there had been some seriously weird things going on in Raven's Cliff recently. The mayor's daughter had been blown off a cliff on her wedding day, for cripe's sake, and during the search they'd found a different woman, wearing a wedding dress and claiming to be a bride of the sea or some such thing.

But whether or not he thought her town and its inhabitants were on the creepy side, he got where Roxie was coming from. This was her haven, the place she'd picked to make her life. She didn't like thinking that there might be a monster hidden among the people she'd tried so hard to fit in amongst.

In that moment she looked so sad, so lost, that he wanted to go to her, wanted to hold her and tell her everything was going to be okay.

But he couldn't promise that, couldn't promise her anything, so instead he said, "I'll call on the replacement equipment and get it here ASAP. Once we've got it, we'll test everything in the kitchen for contamination, and rule out the possibility that this was deliberate, however far-fetched that idea might seem to some of us. Then we can get back to work on the patient samples and nail this...whatever it is."

She glanced at him, expression hooded. "Tell me you think we'll get a cure developed in time to save these people."

He tipped his head. "We're going to do our absolute best."

But he didn't promise, because it would be a lie.

ROX ARMED HERSELF with the .22 and made a couple of trips into town to load up on bottled water and canned provisions. The replacement equipment didn't arrive until midafternoon, and once it did, it took nearly three hours to set up the machines and get them ready to run the necessary samples.

Luke programmed one of the machines to specifically look for peptide fragments from the enzyme they'd found in the too-large fish, and put Bug on scanning the supplies that they'd stocked into the monastery kitchen when they'd arrived.

Captain Swanson hung around and watched them run the first set of samples. His men had located a handful of teens who'd broken curfew, but the kids swore they'd been swimming in the riptides off Beacon Lighthouse and hadn't been near the monastery. Since riptide diving was forbidden and had earned the kids a stern lecture from Captain Swanson, along with various parental punishments, it seemed like a good bet they hadn't been the ones to trash the lab.

Which left the question of who, exactly, had done it.

In the light of day, Rox went over her former bedroom—now Luke's—a second time, then a third, looking for confirmation of the secret passage that had to be there. She came up empty. She also failed to find an entrance to the supposed secret passageways in the kitchen, even though there should've been an access point there, too. Otherwise, given that the back door through the kitchen had been shut and locked tight, they should've seen the vandals headed through the front when they escaped.

But the more she looked, the more it seemed like the monastery's resident ghosts had been responsible for both her nighttime scare and the vandalism in the field lab.

Frustrated by her inability to find what logic told her had to be there, she headed back to the kitchen. "Any hits?"

Luke shook his head. "Everything's clean so far, at least of the enzyme. Since we don't know what exactly the fish were dosed with in the first place to make them overproduce the enzyme, I can't say for sure. It's more a case that we haven't gotten a positive result, not so much that there's nothing there."

His explanation meant they'd be eating out of cans for the foreseeable future, at least until they identified the initial trigger that was causing the fish to grow so large, overproduce hormones and develop the telltale dark lateral line.

Rox sighed. "Okay. I'm headed out for bed check if anyone's looking for me."

"Will do," Luke said, his attention clearly on the samples and his machines.

Bug shot her a sympathetic look as she passed, making it obvious that Thom had told him about her and Luke's little scene earlier. Which was just great. She loved being the center of gossip. Not.

Shrugging her shoulders beneath her doctor's coat, she headed for the patient area, starting with May.

The clinician didn't look any worse, which was encouraging. Unfortunately, she didn't look any better, either. She was breathing regularly and her vitals were stable, but there was no change in her comatose state. The same was true of the patients in the next three rooms she checked. Even their white counts had stabilized, suggesting that their bodies had reached an equilibrium. Dispirited, Rox entered the fourth room expecting more of the same—nothing good.

It took her a moment to realize that something had changed.

Henry Wylde's heart rate was up, and he had brain wave activity indicative of waking.

Rox's pulse bumped and she felt a little flutter of excitement. Thinking of Henry's wife, Mary, and their two young children, she crossed her fingers that he was coming around. He'd been one of the first nonviolent patients to get sick.

Now, maybe he'd be the first to wake up.

Trying not to picture the joy of being able to tell Mary that her husband was on the mend, Rox crossed to him and touched his wrist. "Henry? Can you hear me?"

She got no outward response, but the EEG spiked slightly, indicating that his brain had perceived the sound, at the very least.

"You got something?" Thom asked from the doorway.

Rox nodded, cautious excitement bubbling. "The EEG says his brain's coming back online."

"I'll get Luke."

Moments later, Luke strode in, crossed to the bed and ran through Henry's vitals. Then he leaned close. "Henry? You ready to open your eyes for us?"

Henry's eyelids quivered, and slowly, he opened his eyes. But he didn't fix on Luke's face, just stared blankly.

Luke clicked on a penlight, checked the pupillary response and shook his head when he didn't get the expected contraction. "I need you to follow the light for me."

Nothing. The EEG suggested Henry was awake and registering Luke's commands. But he wasn't responding to them.

Rox's elation drained and she sucked in a breath, and when Luke glanced up and met her eyes, she saw the same worry in him.

Henry wasn't on the mend at all. He was in the next stage of the disease: a waking coma.

Worse, as they watched, his EEG grew erratic for a moment, then smoothed out. Stuttered. Smoothed. His brain was firing randomly in burst patterns that meant nothing.

"That is not good," Bug said from behind Rox, and she nodded numbly, tears filling her eyes, because burst firing didn't mean the patient was waking up.

It meant his brain was shutting down.

AFTER THEY'D CHECKED the rest of the patients—finding no change in any of the others—Luke assembled his team in the kitchen.

Or rather, his team plus Rox, he reminded himself.

There was no sense in getting used to having her around, because she wasn't "around." He just happened to be in her space for the moment. When he moved on, she'd stay put in the place she'd decided to call home.

He wanted to ask her why she'd choose a gloomy, slightly shabby fishing village when she could've kept traveling, or picked anywhere in the world to settle down. When she'd left Africa, she'd had offers from some of the most prestigious hospitals and private practices in the country—he knew, because he'd phoned in the recommendations himself, trying to give her what he could when he couldn't give her what she'd wanted from him.

Yet with all those opportunities, she'd moved to Raven's Cliff, which he just didn't get.

Not your business, he reminded himself yet again. *Her choice. Her life.*

"We need to work faster," she said now, not waiting for him to get the meeting started in his role as team leader. "Henry doesn't have much time left, and if the disease runs true to pattern, the others won't be far behind him."

Her hazel eyes were dark with grief and underscored with the faint bruises of fatigue that said she was pushing herself too hard, taking the work too personally. At least that was what he'd told her time and again when they'd been on assignment together. He couldn't very well tell her not to take it personally this time, though, because for her it *was* personal. For that matter, it had become personal for him and his team, too.

May might be days behind the other patients in her disease progression, but so far she'd gone through all the same phases. If they died, she would die—unless he figured out the nature of the toxin, and came up with an antidote before then.

"I'm not sure what else we can do," he said after a moment of tired, dispirited silence. "We've sent out the samples, and are running all the field tests possible. We've tried feeding the enzyme to normal fish and got nothing, so that's a by-product, not the actual trigger. What else do you suggest?"

"I don't know." Rox's shoulders sagged under the weight of the people she cared for, most of whom didn't seem to give a flip about her.

"What about giving a shout out to the Cod Project?" Bug said, seeming hesitant. "I know it's a long shot, but they might be able to help."

Luke frowned. "The what?"

But Rox was ahead of him. "Someone's sequencing the codfish genome?"

The geneticist nodded. "They want to use it to help select fish that'll do well for aquaculture—you know, fish farming. Brood stock development, that sort of thing."

"Do you think they'd be willing to sequence the DNA of one of our overgrown fish?" Luke asked, starting to get interested. "See if there's a mutation that's causing the enzyme overproduction?"

But Bug shook his head. "That'd take way too long. Besides, we have no reason to believe the DLD is a mutation—we're only seeing the enlarged growth and lateral stripe in adult fish in the prime of life, not juveniles or seniors, suggesting it's not being passed on genetically. And even if it were based on a genetic change and we compared the DNA of our fish to those of the reference genome at the Cod Project, it'd be impossible to tell which DNA differences are important to the disease and which are just natural variations."

Rox blew out a breath. "So we just talked ourselves out of using the cod genome."

"Not necessarily." Bug leaned in, his eyes lighting with what Luke recognized as his "I think I've got a decent idea" look. "We can use subtractive RNA hybridization." At the baffled looks of the others, he explained, "If you think of DNA as the blueprint of a cell, then RNA is the guy who explains the blueprints to the construction crews. When a cell wants to make a protein—or do pretty much anything—it translates the relevant DNA into a strand of RNA, and the RNA guides production."

"Which helps us how?" Luke asked.

"If we isolate all of the RNA from the cells of normal and DLD fish, label the strands with different fluorescent tags and then mix them under conditions that tell the RNA to stick to other copies of itself," Bug said, "then whatever's left over is the stuff that doesn't match. If we clone and sequence those strands, the folks at the Cod Project should be able to tell us what the RNA encodes."

Rox frowned. "Sounds involved. How long will it take to get an answer?"

"If we get lucky? A day or two." Bug lifted a shoulder. "If not? Weeks, maybe months. The luck factors into how many different genes are differentially regulated by whatever's causing the DLD, and whether we sequence the right one immediately. Growth is a complicated process. We might have to wade through a whole lot of genes before we get to the culprit."

Luke cursed under his breath, thinking that there had to be an easier way to figure out what the hell was causing the strange symptoms. But he also knew it was better to get the time-consuming experiments started sooner than wish he had later.

"We'll do it," he said finally. "Bug and Thom, you put together a supply list and we'll get right on it." He looked around the table, skipping over May's empty spot and trying not to think of her lying in the narrow cot, with the IV drip-drip-dripping into her vein. "Anything else?"

"Just more negatives," Bug said. "I've tested everything I can think of from the kitchen, and haven't gotten a hit on the enzyme yet. I've got one more set of samples to go." He glanced at his watch. "Speaking of which…"

He rose and crossed to the lab side of the kitchen just as the peptide sequencer beeped to indicate the end of a run.

Drawn by the lure of data, Luke rose and joined him, as did Thom and Rox moments later. All three of them leaned over Bug's shoulder as he tapped a few keys on the computer screen, bringing up the results.

Bug's eyes went wide. "Hello."

Luke leaned in. "Damn."

Their nondairy coffee creamer was positive for the enzyme being produced by the overlarge fish.

May's disease was no accident or naturally transmitted infection. It was attempted murder.

THIS TIME WHEN his "investor" called, Wells was ready for him. He picked up the handset. "I have good news."

There was a pause, then the carefully modulated voice said, "Oh?"

"I snuck a couple of listening devices into the monastery when the doctors were setting up the other day, and I've been doing some eavesdropping. They're not looking anywhere near the FDA licenses. They're convinced it's the fish—something about dark lines and DNA. I didn't get all of it."

"Did you record everything?"

"Yeah." Wells paused, knowing he had a commodity. "It'll cost you, though."

"E-mail the recording to the usual address. I'll have the money wired to you tomorrow."

"No," the mayor said quickly. "Not money. A promise. Your unconditional support during the next election."

"I don't shill for local politicians." There was a curl of contempt in the voice.

"Not local. The senate."

"Really." There was a long pause before the voice said, "Agreed. That could be beneficial to both of us."

The caller hung up without saying goodbye, but Wells didn't give a crap about that as excitement burgeoned through him. He was dying to get out of this gloomy little town. It was a stepping stone, nothing more.

Today he was a mayor. Tomorrow a senator.

Next stop, the White House.

Chapter Seven

Henry Wylde died the next day, followed twenty hours later by Tony Prentiss. The other nonviolents were traveling the same path, meaning that all of them— even May—would be dead within the next few days if Rox and the others didn't find a cure, an antidote, something.

The Violents, on the other hand, remained comatose. There were some slight changes in EEG activity suggesting a waking state, but they were unresponsive to painful stimuli and other tests of consciousness, indicating that they truly were comatose, not faking it.

Rox mourned the dead, and felt the weight of the town's condemnation. Or maybe that was her own self-directed anger she was feeling—she should've been able to save them, should've been able to find the source of the disease in time, should've been able to figure out a cure.

Logically, she knew that wasn't fair. Luke was the best of the best, and Bug and Thom were solid. Scientists across the country were working on samples from Raven's Cliff and coming up with small pieces of information but no cures. She was only one person, so how could she expect herself to do alone what they hadn't yet managed as a team?

Still, guilt sliced deep and left her bleeding as she did her work mechanically, taking on the majority of patient care while Luke and the others worked on the subtractive RNA hybridization, and Captain Swanson, homicide detective Andrei Lagios and two of the four Chapman brothers, all of whom were members of the RCPD, tried to figure out who had sabotaged the field lab and laced the coffee creamer with the telltale enzyme.

So far they'd all come up empty.

Worse, early on the second morning the peptide sequencer fell from its secure stand and wound up irreparably broken, and the portable refrigerator died, taking a number of important samples with it. It might've just been bad luck. Or it might've been another, more subtle attempt at sabotage. Unable to tell which, and unwilling to risk another piece of equipment—or a teammate—Luke brought in motion detectors and set them up in the kitchen, entryway and halls. That meant the doctors had to deactivate the things when they walked into an area, and reactivate them when they left, even if they were just passing through.

It was an added layer of protection, granted, but the aggravation wore on Rox and the members of the CDC team until, by the second night, the air had grown stiff with tension, and all of their tempers were frayed.

Luke, Rox, Bug and Thom met for dinner. It was a silent affair broken only by desultory conversation about the patients' status—unchanged—and the progress of the investigations—not much.

"What we're doing isn't working," Rox finally said. "We need a new angle on this thing."

"Like what?" Luke snapped. "Faith healing? Face it, we're doing everything we can. Science takes the time it takes, and nobody promised we'd be able to solve this thing in a week."

"Well, that's all the time we have," she countered, feeling anger spike alongside frustration. "You may not care about the people in my 'creepy little town'— that's what you've been calling it, right?—but I'd like to think you care about your own teammate. If we don't figure out what those fish were dosed with in the next day or so, May is going to die."

Luke slapped his palms on the table and lunged to his feet, bending to glare at her over the table that separated them. "You think I don't get that? You think I don't care about what's happening to May?"

She met his glare with one of her own. "It's hard to think otherwise when you barely even look at her room—never mind going in there—unless you absolutely, positively have to. Seems to me the moment she got sick, you wrote her off."

At that, Thom and Bug started looking uneasy, like they wished they were somewhere else. But when Bug started to rise, Luke waved him back into place. "No, stay. We're in this together, so we might as well clear the air." He bared his teeth, eyes glinting as he leaned even closer to Rox. "This isn't about me and May at all, is it? It's about you and me. You think I've checked out on May the same way I checked out on you."

She forced herself to hold her ground, hating to do this in front of his coworkers, but not sure doing it in private would've been an improvement. "I think you've checked out on this entire case. You're going through the motions, finishing up the hybridization but not starting anything new. We're not brainstorming, we're not trying new treatments that 'just might work.' You've got us hunkering down until the last of the nonviolent patients dies."

He straightened away from the table with a curse. "That's ridiculous."

But she heard it in his voice, saw it in the way he wouldn't meet her eyes, and her insides chilled. "That's it, isn't it? You're wrapping things up. You're leaving."

Bug and Thom glanced at Luke, startled. "No way, boss," Thom said. "Right?"

Luke grimaced. "The outbreak isn't really an outbreak—it's more of a police matter at this point. And it's not like we're making progress here. We can do more with the samples back at the CDC lab than we can here. We can liaise with the feds easier, coordinate the reverse engineering of whatever toxin or contaminant triggered the fish response, and figure out how it turns into DLD in humans. All of that will be easier from D.C."

That was true, Rox supposed, but it all boiled down to one thing. "You're running again," she said softly. "The answers aren't easy, the heroism isn't quick, so you're running."

She expected anger from him. Instead, he said, "It's not safe for you here, and it won't be until Swanson and the others figure out who contaminated the fish, and why." A pause. "Come back to D.C. with us. You can work the case from my lab."

It was a startling offer, and to some degree a tempting one. She'd have access to state-of-the-art equipment and lightning-fast results, along with a collection of medical minds second to none. And there was a piece of her that wanted to think the invitation had something to do with the sharp awareness between them, the heat that flared with the casual brush of a hand in the hallway, the lock of eyes across the room.

But even if that was the case, what was the point? She'd be coming back on his terms, not her own.

Been there, done that, didn't work.

So she shook her head. "I'm staying."

"You're clinging," he corrected. "Again." He got in her face and the heat that rose between them wasn't sexual chemistry this time. It was anger. Frustration. "You think I'm running? Well you're no better—you're clinging to a group of people who don't want your help and couldn't care less if you disappeared tomorrow, just like you clung to our relationship long after it should've been pronounced dead."

A fiery wash of embarrassment poured through Rox, flushing her face and making her want to jump up and hurry away, lock herself in her room. But that would be running, which was his style, not hers.

So instead, she rose to her feet so she could match him glare for glare. "I'd rather cling to a lost cause than run away from something unfinished."

When he didn't say anything, she lifted her chin and turned away. "Sorry you got dragged into that one," she said to Bug and Thom, and stalked from the room.

That was a strategic retreat. Not running.

She deactivated the motion detectors in the entryway and west wing, and reset them once she was at the door to her room. Then, feeling marginally safe and so tired and heart-sore it almost didn't matter, she hit the lights and climbed into her cot.

And was asleep in minutes, faint tear tracks drying on her cheeks.

LUKE ALMOST WENT after Rox when she barged out of the kitchen. He didn't, though, because what was the point? Maybe some of what she'd said was right, but he'd been right, too.

They might be at a dead end with the investigation, but the way to mix things up wasn't to keep brainstorming things they could do from Raven's Cliff, it was to go back to the main lab and be scientists.

She didn't seem to get that fieldwork was only a part of what he did these days. He spent a good chunk of his time at a damn desk. Hell, he'd even bought a condo.

Exhaling a long, frustrated breath, he turned to Thom and Bug. "I'm sorry about that, too. Things between Rox and me were never exactly quiet and peaceful. But I'm serious about it being time to go home. I'll—"

He broke off when he realized they weren't looking at him sympathetically.

They were glaring.

"What?"

Bug shook his head, disgusted. "She's right. You've checked out on May, and we let you. Well, guess what? That's over, starting now. We're staying right here, and we're going to come up with some new treatment ideas, the crazier the better."

"I'm not checking out on anybody," Luke snapped. "I'm being a realist. And you know what the reality is? Sometimes people die when you don't want them to.

It's not right and it's not fair, but it's the truth. Holding on to them, fighting for them…it's just a waste of effort. I'd far rather concentrate on the things I *can* change rather than the ones I can't."

Thom's expression went sad. "Then I pity you, dude. If you're not fighting for something—or someone—then what's the point?"

"The point," Luke snarled, "is that we came here to do a job, which was to support the local medical professional in an outbreak situation, identify the pathogen or toxin and take measures to prevent the spread or reoccurrence of the issue."

When the others didn't interrupt, he ticked off the points on his fingers. "One, in a few more days, Rox is going to be down to a few Violent patients who aren't contagious, and who seem stable enough for transport to a secure facility. Two, we've done what we can on the identification front—we may have to leave the details up to the feds and the Fish and Game Department."

He added a third finger for his final point. "And three, we've done the best we can with our containment and prevention measures. The locals are going to catch and destroy all the large fish they can find, and whatever's going on with those fish, it doesn't seem to be passed on to their offspring. Once the locals have taken care of the DLD fish currently out there, there shouldn't be another case of the human disease."

Thom shook his head. "You're assuming there won't be any new cases of contamination, but that doesn't play. Someone's been sabotaging our efforts so we can't uncover an antidote. That suggests he—or she—intends to continue using the contaminant for some purpose." He paused. "It also suggests that Rox is going to be in even more danger if we leave. You don't really think she's going to stop investigating because we're gone, do you?"

"I asked her to come with us," Luke growled through clenched teeth, not sure how he'd become the bad guy here.

"And she turned you down," Thom countered. "So what are you going to do about it?"

Luke glared at his biochemist. "I'm not going to do anything about it," he said, hating the twist in his gut that came with making the most logical decision. "She's an adult, and she can make her own choices, no matter how screwed up I think they are." He gathered up his dinner dishes, along with Rox's, and dumped them in the sink, signaling that the discussion was over. "We start wrapping things up in the morning."

Thom stood and said with quiet defiance, "If you take off, you're going without me." He left the room without another word.

Luke cursed under his breath, then turned to Bug. "What about you?"

The stocky, bearded geneticist nodded. "Sorry. I'm staying, too. But that's not really the point here."

"Oh?" Luke arched an eyebrow, warning the other man to tread carefully. "And what, precisely, is the point if it's not about the mutiny of my so-called team?"

"The point is that Rox is right about one thing. You owe May better than this. She trusted you to keep her safe, and she got sick instead. Running away from that isn't going to make it better. If anything, it's going to make it worse. You either come to terms with your responsibility there, or it's going to haunt you for the rest of your life."

The breath backed up in Luke's lungs and a heavy weight settled in his chest, making him feel as if he was suffocating. "That's not fair."

"Neither is the fact that she's dying," Bug said bluntly. He stood and gathered up the rest of the dishes, dumping them in the sink to soak until one of them got around to cleanup. On his way out of the kitchen, he lobbed a parting shot. "Any one of us would've done better by you."

And the hell of it was, Luke thought as Bug strode from the room, he was right. They all were—not about staying and fighting a losing battle, but about his responsibility to May.

She'd trusted him, and he'd let her down, just like he'd let Rox down before.

That was why he tried to keep his friendships on the surface and fleeting. If he wasn't around people for long, he could be what they expected him to be— strong and smart and a hell of a doctor. It was only later that the cracks started to show.

Standing alone in the monastery kitchen, with tens of thousands of dollars of field equipment humming nearby, he cursed bitterly, wishing things could be different, wishing *he* could be different.

He wished he could be the man Rox wanted him to be, the leader his teammates expected him to be. He wished he could be the doctor that the residents of Raven's Cliff needed.

And maybe a small piece of him wished he hadn't intercepted Rox's cry for help, hadn't muscled his way into the investigation when she'd specifically tried to exclude him. Because if he hadn't come to Raven's Cliff, hadn't gotten himself neck-deep in a case that was far more complicated and dangerous than any of them had anticipated, he wouldn't be where he was now—all stirred up, with one of his team members in a coma and the other two furious with him, and Rox...

She was furious with him, too, and with good reason. If he hadn't come back, their relationship could've stayed dead and buried. Another team would've taken the outbreak, with probably the same level of success and far less interpersonal drama.

So why had he come back?

He didn't know. And he wasn't figuring it out— wasn't figuring anything out—standing in the kitchen. He told himself to go to bed, told himself to shut it off for a few hours and let his subconscious mind percolate the things that his conscious mind was having no luck with.

Instead, he headed for the auto-sampler and the attached laptop computer, and pulled up all the data they'd amassed so far on the fish enzyme and human DLD. He opened up a new spreadsheet and started plugging in details, then moved them around, poking at the information, trying to make it fall into a new pattern...hell, any pattern at all.

He was still at it three hours later when the motion detectors shrilled to life and all hell broke loose.

THE ALARMS YANKED ROX from a deep sleep, and it took her a moment to orient. When she did, when she heard shouting, and footsteps pounding out in the hallway just beyond the door to her room, fear jolted through her, hard and hot.

What was going on out there?

She struggled up from her cot, hit the light switch to illuminate her room and then jammed her feet into her shoes, jerking the laces tight. She was at the unlocked door, brandishing her heavy flashlight when the doorknob turned and the heavy panel burst inward.

Aztec Wheeler stood in the doorway, eyes blazing red with anger and disease. His expression lit with terrible glee when he saw her. *"Roxanne."*

Rox screamed and backpedaled, trying to get away from him as he lurched into the narrow room, arms outstretched, repeating her name over and over again in a guttural, growling voice.

She slammed into the far wall beside the barred window, and her heart clutched. Aztec was between her and the door, and there wasn't another way out.

The hallway was in chaos, with shambling figures running back and forth, wearing hospital jonnies and roaring curses and pleas. All of the Violents were up and moving, and they'd gotten loose!

"Roxanne, Roxanne, my Roxanne," Aztec crooned horribly as he advanced on her. "Pretty, pretty Roxanne."

She thought she heard Luke shout her name, and heard the *whiz-zap* of his Taser out in the hallway, but knew he'd be too late, if he got to her at all.

"Get away from me!" she shouted at Aztec, and threw the flashlight with all her strength.

He didn't duck, and the missile caught him in the eye, impacting with a solid clunk. He howled and reeled back, grabbing for his face. In backpedaling, he tangled with the contents of her suitcase, which were still strewn on the floor because she hadn't had time to organize.

Roaring, he tripped and went down, smacking his head on the edge of the cot.

Heart pounding, Rox took the momentary distraction and bolted past him, headed for the door, for freedom, for—

He snagged her ankle and yanked, and she fell face-first, slamming her chin on the unforgiving stone floor. The impact dazed her for a moment, making the room spin as he dragged her backward by her ankle, moving his grip to her calf, her thigh.

Rox screamed and fought. She heard gunshots from the hallway, and the sound of more shouts and footsteps, though she didn't know if they were from friend or foe.

"Luke, *help me!*" she cried, unable to get any leverage as Aztec rolled her onto her back and loomed over her, his body hard and hot against hers, leaving no question as to his intent, only the question of whether he'd kill her before or after.

She arched her body beneath his, scrabbling with her hands, trying to find leverage, a weapon, something, anything.

"I like it when you scream." Aztec grinned horribly, wrapped one strong fisherman's hand around her neck and squeezed.

She gurgled and strained, grabbing at his hand and trying to pry it away as she struggled for air, for life. Her vision went gray and her pulse pounded in her ears, hard and erratic.

Luke! she screamed in her mind when she couldn't get the cry past the hand closing her throat.

Aztec moved to straddle her, his heavy weight pressing on her chest and lungs, his too-strong hand choking her. His eyes were alight with excitement, along with something that looked disconcertingly like love. "Roxanne, Roxanne," he crooned in a singsong growl. "My Roxanne."

As the gray haze went dark, she saw movement in the doorway. Seconds later came the crack of gunfire.

Aztec stiffened, got a surprised look on his rage-contorted face and collapsed atop her, his hand going slack on her throat.

Rox thrashed as the warm wetness of his blood seeped onto her and a thin trickle of oxygen entered her lungs, but he was too heavy. He was crushing her, suffocating her even in death. "Help," she gasped. "Get him off!"

Then Luke was there, hauling Aztec off her and dragging her up, clutching her in his arms so tightly she still couldn't breathe, not because she was suffocating, but because she was holding on just as tight.

She pressed her face into the crook of his neck, breathing and sobbing and shuddering, and he held her, just held her, seeming as solid as the stone around them.

"It's okay," he said, voice shaky. "I've got you. Hang on, I've got you." He pulled her up and away from Aztec's body, and guided her out of the room, shutting the door at their backs.

The hallway was empty now, but there was evidence of the brief war that had been waged. The wireless motion detectors had been torn down and lay in splintered pieces on the floor. There was a small blood spatter on the wall and a streak of the red liquid farther down, and at least one of the Violents' doors was lying flat on the floor, like it'd been smashed outward by some terrible force.

As they headed toward the entryway, Rox's head cleared and she began to believe that she was away from Aztec, that Luke really had rescued her by killing a man.

"How did they get loose?" she asked in a trembling voice, turning to look back at the farthest set of rooms, where the Violent patients had been locked. Only the one door had been battered down. The rest stood open. "Did you catch them all?" She caught her breath as a horrible thought occurred. "Are the nonviolents okay?"

What if the Violents had gotten at Jeff and Wendy? What if they'd killed May?

"The other patients are fine," Luke said quickly, steering her toward the entryway.

Bug and Thom were there, looking bruised and battered but alive. Several of Swanson's officers were there, too, breathing heavily and looking wild-eyed, like they couldn't believe what they'd just experienced. Jenks and Jake Welstrom lay facedown, their arms and legs cuffed as they squirmed and swore, and cast red-eyed glares around the room.

"Aztec?" Thom asked quietly.

Luke shook his head. "He's dead," he said bleakly. "I had no choice."

There was a moment of profoundly uncomfortable silence, broken only by the curses of the two restrained men.

"What happened?" Rox finally whispered, because none of it made any sense at all. The Violents had been nonresponsive for so long, and they'd all gotten sick at different times, making it illogical that they would all come around simultaneously.

"They were faking it," Thom said. "Or else someone was drugging them to keep them down until it was time to bust them loose."

"Impossible," Luke said dismissively. "An intruder would've tripped the motion detectors."

"Not if he was using secret passageways," Rox countered.

He looked down at her, faint frustration crinkling his brow. "Which would be a good explanation…if we could prove they exist."

Realizing she was still burrowed into his arms, she pulled away, though she stayed close to him, drawing strength from the knowledge that he was at his best in a crisis.

"We should look again," she said. "Organize a real search, and bring in some equipment."

"We'll take care of that," Captain Swanson announced, appearing in the front entryway with the dark of a gloomy, foggy night behind him. "You doctors have other things to worry about."

Thom's face fell. "You didn't catch Doug Allen."

Rox's gut knotted at the news that a Violent who'd already killed two innocent victims was on the loose.

"That's not the only problem," the police chief reported. He waved behind him, to the front parking area, where numerous engines rumbled, one of them the low-throated growl of a big truck, or a bus. "We got here so quickly because we were already on our way. You've got more patients. Lots more."

Luke cursed and crossed the entryway to look out, with the others on his heels. Rox gasped when she saw the number of fog-shrouded police cars, each with two or three people locked in the back. "How many?" she whispered.

"Thirty-two at last count," Swanson replied. "We're doing another house-to-house now."

"How many Violents?" Luke demanded.

"That's the strange thing. None." The police chief scowled. "If I were an optimist, I'd say that was good news. But given what's been going on around here, and the fact that we've got nearly fifteen people currently unaccounted for around town, I'm thinking it's a bad sign."

Luke nodded. "I'm with you."

One of the other cops frowned. "Why is it bad? Doesn't the lack of violent patients mean that the disease is losing steam?"

"No," Rox said softly. "It means whoever broke out our Violents tonight has already collected the others. He's building himself an army."

But why? And how could they stop him?

Chapter Eight

The doctors worked through the night getting the new patients settled, and watched them descend into catatonia despite all efforts to counter the progression of the toxic response.

Each time another patient went still, Luke's tension ratcheted up another notch. He was a toxicologist, damn it, and he was supposed to be a hotshot. He sure as hell ought to be able to figure this out.

So he left the others to sleep in shifts and tend the patients under round-the-clock police protection, and went back to work in the field lab.

He was on to something. Maybe.

The preliminary results from the subtractive hybridization were a mishmash of growth-related genes and stress-related proteins, any of which could reasonably be turned on by the effects of whatever change had kicked the growth into high gear.

The question was, which one among them was the starting point, the change that sat at the apex of the genetic response? What was the damn trigger?

He found a clue in an e-mail from a scientist at the

Cod Project, identifying the genes from their last round of subtractive hybridization.

One of the genes had been identified as: *Unnamed open reading frame, designated Cod Project 12.21*. What was interesting was the appended note, which read: *frmshft del 4bp*.

Luke knew enough to identify that as meaning there was a frameshift mutation, in which four base-pairs of DNA had been deleted from the normal gene.

He wasn't sure why Bug—who was the geneticist on the team—hadn't picked up on the note. Maybe it had something to do with how much time he'd been spending at May's bedside, looking more and more haggard as the hours passed and her EEG started to show signs of the waking coma that preceded death.

Luke's anger upped a notch. Someone was trying to kill his people, and the residents of Raven's Cliff. That was the only logical explanation for the sudden rash of new cases. The bastard had dosed the victims with something tainted—the water supply, or an aerosol spray. Luke didn't know whether this was some sort of twisted clinical trial, or a madman's efforts to create an army of violent human beings without inhibition or self-control. Either way it was diabolical. Terrible.

And Rox was smack in the middle of it.

"Come on, come on," he muttered to the DNA sequencer as the machine did its thing. He'd isolated DNA from all the overgrown fish they'd collected, along with all the normal controls, and now he was testing to see if the frameshift mutation was present in every one of the altered fish and absent from every one of the controls. While that didn't explain how the mutation had occurred, if he'd found the gene that turned on production of the aberrant hormone in the fish, maybe they could reverse-engineer a protein that would nullify the effect of the overproduced enzyme.

In theory, anyway. And right now, theory was all he had to go on, because none of the usual protocols had done them any good.

Moments later the computer dinged to indicate that it had finished the sequencing runs. He clicked through, telling the software to analyze the fluorescence-based data and display it on-screen.

A few moments after that, he stuck his head into the entryway and shouted, "Bug! Get in here!"

When the geneticist skidded into the kitchen, wide-eyed, he was clearly expecting to find that more equipment had been sabotaged. "What? What's wrong?"

"Nothing. For a change, something might actually be right." Luke gestured at the screen. "Take a look."

Bug looked. And whistled. "Nice going, boss."

He tapped a few keys, sat down at the computer, and tapped a few more. Within a minute, he was instant-messaging with his buddy at the Cod Project, while simultaneously searching several genome databases for genes that might be related to CP 12.21.

"If we can figure out what this puppy does," he said, "we should be able to come up with something to block the enzyme."

Luke clapped him on the shoulder. "Get on it. I'm going to check on the patients." He headed out, but turned back when Bug called his name. "Yeah?"

"Does this mean we're staying?"

"Yeah," Luke said without a moment's hesitation. "We're not letting this bastard win."

He wasn't sure when he'd made the choice, but

there it was, fully formed inside him. He wasn't giving up on May, wasn't leaving Rox. He didn't know how he'd ever considered it, or what he'd been thinking.

This wasn't about reunions or old arguments that still held true. It was about a murderer who'd targeted an entire town. It was about justice, and making the killer pay for what he'd done.

And it was about making up, as best he could, for leaving Rox behind.

BY NIGHTFALL, Rox was exhausted, both physically and emotionally. She took a short break in May's room, sitting in the bedside chair where Bug spent most of his free time, and closed her eyes. Her bones ached with fatigue, and her heart hurt from the emotional backlash of the newest outbreak.

She'd helped the others set up the new patients on the best supportive therapy they could muster, and then she'd talked to the families, eventually identifying produce from Coastal Fish as being the most likely source of the toxin.

It looked like the bastard had sprayed purified enzyme over all the fruits and vegetables on display. The people who'd gotten sick were those who'd eaten the fruits or veggies raw, without washing them first. Upon learning that, Rox had brought back samples for testing, and when they'd turned up positive for the fish enzyme, she'd contacted Mayor Wells and asked him to have the market pull all their produce and put out a notice that any foods not in bottles or cans should be thoroughly washed before consumption, preferably washed and cooked.

The mayor had agreed, and seemed genuinely concerned. But Rox couldn't help thinking that, like his everyday persona, the concern had been too polished, too slick.

Or maybe that was just her natural aversion to men who seemed too good to be true.

Case in point was Luke. After his threat of the night before, when he'd acted as if it was perfectly reasonable for him to take his team and head for the hills, he'd done a complete one-eighty and now seemed committed to figuring out an antidote for the enzyme, or its toxin trigger.

He and Bug had spent most of the afternoon with their heads together, cobbling together something they were calling "anti-CP 12.21," after the gene that appeared to be mutated in the affected fish.

Rox wanted to be grateful for Luke's abrupt about-face, and the renewed energy he was pouring into the case, but she was having trouble finding the gratitude. Instead, she found herself wondering how long it would last, and she feared she already knew the answer.

When May died, Luke would be in the wind. And the way Rox figured it, they had eighteen, maybe twenty-four hours before that occurred.

She didn't know what had happened in the past to give Luke such an aversion to seeing someone he knew having trouble with an illness. Logic said he'd lost a family member to a terminal illness—a parent, perhaps, or a sibling. Logic also said the experience was probably why he'd gone in to medicine.

But that was where logic broke down, because if he'd gone into medicine to help prevent things like he'd experienced earlier in life, why would the identity of the patient matter one bit?

"And I'm entirely too tired to figure this out tonight," she said aloud, scrubbing both hands across her tight-feeling face. She looked over at May's still form, automatically cataloging the EEG activity, which was holding steady for the moment, thank God. "I'm going to catch a few hours. I'll check on you first thing when I'm up."

She didn't know if the other woman could hear her, but felt like she needed to say something. It could too easily have been her lying there, dying. If she'd gone for her morning tea before doing rounds that morning—

Don't think about it, she admonished herself. *Get some sleep.*

But when she got to her room, she found it'd gained a motion detector facing the barred window and far corner, along with a second cot and a carefully packed duffel bag that was all too familiar.

The sight of Luke's neatness beside her clutter grabbed her by the heart and twisted as the past and present threatened to collide, with messy results.

It'd been five days since he'd arrived in Raven's Cliff, and for the most part she'd come to grips with him being there, because he'd been right when he'd told her flat-out that he hadn't changed, and neither had she.

Unfortunately, that went both ways. The differences were the same, making it impossible for them to exist as a couple. But at the same time, the things she had once liked—and yes, loved—about him were the same, too.

He was still larger than life, a handsome daredevil

who walked into armed encampments and terrible infectious conditions with aplomb, his casual elegance easing the fears of those around him. He was still hell on wheels as a diagnostician, still ran his team with ruthless efficiency while giving his teammates their own mental space.

He was good at what he did—one of the best—and for that reason alone she couldn't regret that he'd come to Raven's Cliff. Though they had yet to conquer the myriad problems facing them, she didn't want to think about what might've happened if a lesser team leader had responded to her cry for help.

Whether she liked it or not, he truly was a hero, a savior. And he was, quite simply, the hottest guy she'd ever met or wanted to meet. She'd dreamed of him long after they'd said goodbye, and she hadn't found a man who even came close to lighting her up the way he could, not in two years of desultory dates with "I'll call you" endings.

And for that very reason, there was no way in hell she was sharing a bedroom with him, two cots or not.

She spun, intending to march out and have a "no way in hell" discussion with him. She stalled when she found him standing in the doorway, eyes hooded.

"It's a safety precaution," he said before she had a chance to open her mouth. "Swanson couldn't get more motion detectors in until tomorrow, so I want us to sleep in shifts, two to a room, with the last serviceable electronic eye guarding the back of the room and a pair of cops in the hall."

"I don't think—" She broke off because he was already moving across the room and dropping down on his cot. "Hey!"

"Roxie," he said, and his voice sounded unutterably weary. "I know it's not the best answer, but it's the only one I've got right now. I'm doing the best I can, and it's not good enough. I get that. But could we just shut it off for a few hours and resume hostilities in the morning? I'm beat."

Normally, she would've bristled at the implication that she was the one picking fights, but something in his voice gave her pause. Beneath the weariness, she sensed a sadness she'd never known from him before, one that suggested he was feeling the deaths—and the gathering hopelessness—just as much as she was.

Granted, May was one of his, and he had to be grieving over her decline whether he pretended otherwise or not. But this was more, like the whole case had become personal to him on a level that, as far as she knew, he'd always avoided in the past.

When she'd first seen him again after so long, she'd thought she detected a new, darker layer to him. Now, she wondered if this was it, if he'd finally realized that it wasn't about each new village, each new case. It was about the people *in* each new village, and the names behind the cases.

"Don't look at me like that," he said softly, bringing his eyes up to meet hers.

She was still standing near the open door, through which she could see one of their police guards standing his post. Without a word, she swung the door shut. "Don't look at you like what?"

"Like you see something in me that doesn't exist." He held out a hand as though inviting her closer, but his expression went hard. "I told you before—"

"You haven't changed," she interrupted. "I know.

Heard you the first time. Which leaves me wondering who you're trying to convince, me or yourself?"

"Roxie." His voice went to a warning growl when she closed the distance between them. "Be certain before you start something you don't want to finish—whether it be a fight or something else. I don't have much left in me right now."

"I'm not certain of anything at the moment," she said honestly. "Except for one thing. You're tired, I'm tired, and you're right that there's safety in numbers."

She leaned past him and armed the motion detector, which faced away from them so it wouldn't pick up their nighttime movements, but would catch anyone approaching from the window or the corners of the room, where there might or might not be a secret passageway.

Then she returned to the light switch and looked at him. "I say we call it a night, boss. Sound good?"

She flicked off the light at his nod, and retraced her steps to her cot, moving easily around her scattered things. Kicking off her shoes, she lay down, trying not to think that in the narrow room, crammed with two cots along the long sides of the space, they were no farther apart than if they'd been on opposite sides of a king-sized bed.

"Good night, Luke," she said, trying to pretend he was just another colleague, that this was just fieldwork, nothing more.

"'Night, Roxie," he said, sounding more relaxed than he had moments earlier, as though killing the lights had left him free to let down his guard a degree. "And Roxie?"

"Yeah?"

"I'm not, and have never been, the boss of you."

She smiled a little in the darkness. "Try to keep that in mind when the sun comes up, will you?"

LUKE SLEPT BETTER than he'd expected—better, in fact, than he had in a long, long time. Maybe it was exhaustion finally catching up to him, maybe the relief of having a breakthrough with the fish gene.

Or maybe it was simply the sense of not being alone, the steady rhythm of another person's breathing nearby.

He told himself it didn't have anything to do with Roxie, couldn't have anything to do with her, but the assurances rang false, and as the drizzly day dawned, he lay on his side and looked at her, watching her sleep.

The wan light washed the color from the morning, leaving everything in shades of gray. She lay on her side facing him, so they were mirror images of each other, separated by a small strip of stone floor. Her hands were folded beneath her cheek, and the long eyelashes that framed her hazel eyes when she was awake now lay fanned across her delicate skin.

How many other times had he woken ahead of her, and just lay there watching her sleep? Too many to count, though she wouldn't have known that because he'd never told her, had always pretended to be just waking when she did.

Now, as she stirred, he roused himself and climbed from his cot. Deactivating the motion detector, he grabbed his shoes and tiptoed around her scattered belongings to let himself out of the room.

Sleeping together—albeit platonically—had been

jarringly intimate. They didn't need to wake up together, too.

But as he did morning rounds, he couldn't stop thinking of the peace on her face as she'd slept. The trust. And as he met with Bug and Thom, who reported on their progress with the reverse-engineering, he couldn't get Rox's soft voice out of his mind.

He'd been around her less than a week and already she was back under his skin.

"What do you think, boss?" Bug asked, looking at him expectantly.

Luke shook his head in self-disgust. "Sorry, can you say that again? My mind was on something else."

The geneticist gave him a long, considering look, but obliged. "The anti-CP 12.21 is as good as it's going to get. The bench experiments show that it binds selectively to the overproduced enzyme, rendering it nonfunctional." He hesitated. "There's no time to try it in mice or anything. And if anyone higher up finds out that we dosed our patients with a completely untested, unapproved drug…"

He didn't need to finish the sentence. They all knew they were risking their careers with this move.

Luke had done similar things before, using rumored or unproven treatments, even sometimes local remedies with questionable ingredients. But the FDA didn't exactly have power out in the wilds of Africa. In Maine—even in the middle of nowhere of Maine—the regulations were a real concern.

If they gave the anti-CP 12.21 to the patients and it cross-reacted with other, vital proteins in the body, the patients could die.

But if they did nothing, the patients *would* die.

"I'll administer it," Luke said. "That way if it goes wrong, it's on my head."

"You go down, we all go down," Bug said staunchly.

Thom nodded. "We'll do it. Who do you want us to start with? Of the first wave of patients still alive, the older Prentiss kid and his father are the ones who've been sick the longest."

Luke pinched the bridge of his nose weighing his options and not liking any of them. "No," he said finally. "Start with May. She'd want us to."

She was a scientist, and a healer. If she'd been conscious, she would've been the first to volunteer. Now he was stuck doing it for her.

Because it was his decision, and because it could so easily turn out wrong, he held out his hand. "Give me the dose. I'll do it."

Bug looked like he wanted to argue, but at a nudge from Thom, handed over a syringe. "I'd push it slowly, just in case." He paused, starting to look more than a little ill. "We'll be standing by with a crash cart. Just in case."

"Yeah." Luke waited while they gathered the necessary equipment, trying not to make it obvious to the cops that they were doing something that strayed beyond the gray zone of ethics into "somebody stop them" territory.

But the treatment might save her. That was the one thought he kept hold of.

Rox appeared, dressed and ready for the new day, and avoiding his eyes as though she, too, had found it strange that they'd slept in the same room without touching.

Thom brought her up to speed in a few quick sentences, and Luke braced himself for an argument, or worse.

She surprised him by nodding. "I'm in."

The four of them gathered by May's bed, and Rox casually swung the door shut so the cop stationed out in the hall couldn't see what they were doing.

Bug sat in the chair next to the bed and took May's hand in what looked like a habitual gesture, making Luke wonder whether he'd missed something between them before, or if this was a new development…and if the latter, what May would think of it when she awoke.

"Okay, gang. Cross your fingers." Managing for the most part to pretend that the woman in the bed was a stranger, just another patient, Luke pushed the contents of the syringe into the IV line—a little at first, and then a little more when there was no adverse response on any of the monitors.

Gradually, over the course of nearly five minutes, he eased the anti-CP 12.21 into May's bloodstream.

Then they waited. And waited.

Ten minutes turned to fifteen, and there was still no response. May's EEG was still showing the burst activity indicative of shutdown, and her eyes were still open in the end-stage waking coma.

"Damn." Bug stared down at her hand, stroking it over and over again with his thumb. "I thought it was going to work. I really did."

"Science takes the time it takes," Luke reminded him. "Give it a while longer." He headed for the door, though he didn't know where he was going other than out of the room.

"No." The geneticist lowered May's hand with a

pat, and pushed himself to his feet. "I'm going to keep working. There's got to be a way to improve the selectivity, or the activity, or something." He headed out into the hall, mumbling to himself, "Maybe a cofactor. What about—"

"Wait!" Thom shouted. "I see something!"

Rox, who was halfway out the door, spun around, and Bug and Luke crowded back into the room behind her.

"What?" Luke asked, hardly daring to hope. "What did you see?"

"There!" Thom pointed to the EEG, where there was a burst of activity that then went to normal, a burst, then normal.

But Luke saw what he'd seen. "They're slowing down."

As the teammates watched, the telltale bursts of abnormal activity in May's brain slowed, and grew weaker.

"If this keeps up," Bug said quietly, "she'll be back to normal deep sleep patterns in an hour. And then..." He trailed off, because none of them knew what came next.

They could only hope.

"Keep monitoring her," Luke ordered. "Let's see if the improvement continues over the next few hours."

It did. And it didn't.

By lunchtime, May's EEG had stabilized back to the pattern it'd held when she'd first gotten sick. All the tests they ran came up with the same answer: the bad enzyme was all but gone, and her hormones were coming back to normal. By midafternoon, her blood work and other tests were within acceptable limits. As far as the lab tests showed, she should be awake.

But she wasn't.

Bug's eyes were hollow as he stood over her bed. "It's like she's been, I don't know, mentally frozen or something. Like it's voodoo."

"Enough with the haunted house crap," Luke snapped, having heard too much of it lately—from the cops and from his teammates. Heck, even inside his own head. "It's science, pure and simple. We got one enzyme, and that improved things but didn't cure her entirely. That means we missed another physiological response to the toxin." He looked down at May, and almost managed to see her as a medical puzzle rather than a friend. Grasping at that necessary detachment, he said, "There must be another protein—or something—that's out of whack, something other than the enzyme Bug's inhibitor targeted."

He hated saying it, hated knowing it, because of what it meant.

Rox said it for him. "Which means we're back to square one—looking in the patients' blood for something that's off-kilter beyond the hormones, which we've already accounted for."

But it had taken them days to get as far as they had with the enzyme and anti-CP 12.21. May didn't have time for them to start over. None of the patients did.

"Wait," Rox said urgently, "we don't have to go that far back." When the others looked at her, she explained, "May and the second wave of patients were dosed with the enzyme—May in the nondairy creamer, and the others with the toxin sprayed on the produce. They didn't eat mutated fish that were producing the enzyme, so the poisoner had to isolate the enzyme himself and administer it to his victims. We're figuring there's another factor—let's call it 'factor X'—involved in the disease because Bug's inhibitor targets the enzyme, and hasn't been fully effective. But if that's the case, then whoever dosed the nondairy creamer and the produce must've added more than just the enzyme."

Bug's eyes lit. "It must've been a mixture of the enzyme *and* factor X."

"Exactly."

Luke could've kissed her for the mental leap. But beside the kick of excitement at being able to skip several analytic steps was a growing burn of anger, and the realization that they had another avenue to pursue.

So he said, "Thom and Bug, I want you guys to dose the other patients with Bug's inhibitor. Then get started isolating factor X from the tainted foods."

Thom raised an eyebrow, apparently sensing the undercurrent. "Where will you two be?"

Luke took Rox's arm and started steering her toward the door. "We're going to take a drive. I have an idea."

Chapter Nine

Luke didn't say a word until they were in his SUV, heading down the winding monastery driveway. Rox fidgeted in the passenger seat, vaguely uncomfortable with the silence. Or maybe it was being alone with him, too aware of him.

Sleeping in the same room the night before shouldn't have changed anything between them, but it had—for her, at least. Waking up and breathing in his scent, seeing his ruthlessly organized duffel sitting beside the blown-up mess of her suitcase, and pausing over the indentation on his pillow—those were familiar things.

The small details had reminded her of the happy, satisfying times she and Luke had shared—many of them in the bedroom, granted, but a large number in the field, as well. They'd been good together, she remembered, and she felt as if she'd taken some of that back just now by helping Bug and Thom short-cut their isolation of factor X.

She might not be in the field anymore, but she still had the knack.

"Where to?" Luke asked, and she realized he'd stopped at the end of the long driveway.

"It depends on where we're going." She looked at him. "Why, exactly, are we out here while Bug and Thom are doing the lab work?"

His jaw went tight. "Because they don't need me breathing over their shoulders, and there's an avenue we haven't explored sufficiently. One I think you can help me with."

"Which is?"

"Tracking the contamination to its source."

"Oh." Rox sat back in her seat, not sure where the sudden clutch of nerves had come from, but certain she didn't know if this was such a good idea. "Shouldn't we leave that to Captain Swanson?" she said faintly.

Luke shot her a startled look. "You don't want to know who's poisoning your town?"

"I just think we should leave it to the experts." Panic gathered and grew, and she was tempted to jump out of the SUV and head back to the monastery.

"I'm not asking you to be some sort of Mata Hari. Just come into town with me, show me around, tell me all the local gossip. Tell me about this curse."

"That's really not a good idea." She shook her head in an effort to convince both of them. "Whoever has control of this toxin, he's already come after us. Going on the offensive is just going to provoke him."

"You're afraid?" He turned to face her fully. "Since when do you put your own safety in front of your patients'? I remember a couple of times you scared years off my life running into firefights and pulling wounded people to safety, or exposing yourself to infectious agents to get to one last patient, save one last life."

She didn't want to remember those times, or that

woman. Not now, not when he was so close to her. She wanted to tell him she wasn't that person anymore, hadn't been for a long time. But instead she found herself saying softly, "Seems to me you were right there beside me."

"Someone had to watch your back," he said, meeting her eyes. They stared at each other for a moment in silence before he said, "I think what's really going on is that you don't want to think it could be someone you know."

She stiffened, hating that what he'd said struck a chord. "Don't psychoanalyze me."

"Then don't avoid the issue."

"Maybe I just don't want to be alone with you," she said, the words leaving her mouth before she could think them through, or call them back.

"I don't think that's it," he said. "Or if it is, it's because you want it too much, and that's a problem." He held up a hand when she would've protested. "I'm in the same boat, Rox. Last night was… It was familiar. Comfortable. And not as in a boring, old sweatshirt sort of comfortable, but as in the sort of comfort I've missed way more than I realized." He paused, grimacing. "We fit together. It feels right, even though I know it isn't."

"Wow." Rox sat back, surprised by his blunt honesty. But instead of clearing the air between them, it made it worse, because now she knew he was feeling the same way. Warmth sparkled in the air, a physical awareness that went way beyond the physical.

"I know. I'm sorry, I didn't mean to make it even weirder." He tapped the steering wheel. "What I'm saying is that I need you on my team for this one, Rox. I want to help your town, but I can't do it alone."

It was a big admission for a man who prided himself on being *the* man, the go-to guy in any crisis. But still, it wasn't enough. "You broke my heart," she said softly, not looking for sympathy, but needing to say it, needing him to know.

"I'm sorry," he said again, and she believed he truly was—but he still didn't defend himself, still didn't explain why he'd left the way he had.

She was probably going to have to be content with that, she realized. As before, he'd given her as much as he could...and it wasn't enough for her. Still, they had a job to do, and he was right about one thing— despite the heat that flared between them and the temptation to go back where they'd been before, they'd been good together as teammates.

If they banded together now, and set themselves to figuring out who was behind the contamination and the sabotage, she had a feeling they'd succeed. Captain Swanson was hampered by local politics and the preconceptions of a lifelong resident, along with other worries, not the least of which was the high school prom that night, which would happen as scheduled, with the curfew pushed back a few hours.

In contrast, Rox and Luke could focus entirely on the case, and they brought contrasting viewpoints— she loved Raven's Cliff despite, or maybe because of, the eccentricities and superstitions of its residents, while Luke found the town small and creepy, and thought everyone he met had a hidden agenda. Between the two of them, they might be able to figure out who was behind the fish contamination and the DLD, and who was trying to keep them from solving the mystery and healing the town.

"Take a right," she told him, gesturing away from downtown Raven's Cliff. "There's an old mansion out there that was recently bought up by a reclusive millionaire sort. More than a few people are pointing out that the town's troubles didn't kick into high gear until he showed up."

Luke just looked at her for a moment, as though trying to figure out where his head was at, or maybe hers. Then he nodded. "Reclusive millionaire it is." But once they were rolling, he added, "Thank you, Roxie."

She forced herself to focus on the practicalities rather than the tug of longing brought by his deep voice. "Don't thank me until after the tour. I have a feeling we're going to have more suspects than we know what to do with, and not a single shred of evidence in any direction."

THE SEASIDE STRANGLER picked his way along the cliff face beneath the Beacon Lighthouse, his steps sure on the familiar pathway.

There were several entrances to the cave system that only a few knew of, and not even he had mapped all of the Byzantine twists and turns taken by the network of passageways beneath the lighthouse and manor. Today, he chose an entrance he hardly ever used, leading to a series of caves that showed signs of long-ago use in scribblings and firepit remains.

He thought he would do things differently today, varying his usual routine, in the hopes that the sea gods would hear his prayers this time.

The town was dying. Even lovely Roxanne and her friends from the CDC had proven unable to stop the spread of the deadly disease. They were doing their best, but they needed help. His sort of help.

Upon entering the first, larger cave, he lifted the light source he'd carried with him—not a modern flashlight, but an oil lantern he thought might appease the ghost of Captain Earl Raven, master of the curse that haunted Raven's Cliff.

Lighting the wick with a box of matches he'd carried in his pocket, he moved deeper into the caves, drawn by something he couldn't name. He wasn't even sure what he was looking for—a proper place to pray to the sea gods, or a hint of how he could save the town, perhaps.

But when he came to the last cave, where this arm of the system dead-ended, he realized that the sea gods had already answered his prayers.

A tawny-haired woman lay asleep beneath a light blue blanket, chained in place, waiting for him.

"You're here," he said reverently, only then realizing that she was what had drawn him to this cave system.

Gently, with the respect due to a woman like her, he unfastened her chains and lifted her from the cot. Slinging her over his shoulder, he gave thanks to the ghost of Captain Raven, lifted the oil lantern and carried her from the place where he'd found her.

He had a different cave in mind for her preparation, one that would be far more fitting for a Sea Bride...and her sacrifice.

ROX'S GRAND TOUR of Raven's Cliff ended, as she figured was only fitting, at the Beacon Lighthouse. Equally fitting, it was dusk, and the evening fog had rolled in to cloak the scene in eerie blue mist washed with a blush of red sunset.

She directed Luke to park the SUV by the manor house. The manor was a tall, brick-faced monster done in the Federal style popular during the late 1700s when it was built. Set high on a rocky promontory of land, Beacon Manor had been the beginning of Raven's Cliff—the town had grown up around it, generously funded by the wealthy sea captain, Earl Raven.

But it wasn't the manor that drew Rox now, it was the lighthouse beyond, a glorious forty-foot beacon that overlooked pristine, wave-pounded beaches that were closed to swimmers because of the deadly rip-tides.

As she led Luke along the pathway to the sea, he said, "It's a pretty town and all, Rox, but I just don't get the attraction. Don't you miss being out in the field?"

She'd known it was coming, had seen the dismissal in his face as she'd guided him around town, sketching out each of the major players for him and answering his questions as fully as she could, while at the same time trying to get him to see the beauty she found in the way simplicity existed alongside complexity in the seaside community.

"I love it here," she said. "I know who I am here, and I feel like I'm home." But even as she said the words, she realized they jarred faintly, that her usual conviction wasn't there.

The more time she spent with Luke, the more she was remembering the old adventures, the old excitement.

"Come on," she said, leading him around the side of the lighthouse. "We can sit here."

On the seaward side of Beacon Lighthouse, there was a small indentation in the earth where many people had sat over the years. Somehow the cliff side and the shape of the lighthouse combined to create a sheltered spot just there, where the sea breeze and fog didn't go, and the air was a few degrees warmer than elsewhere.

She sat and leaned back against the whitewashed masonry wall of the lighthouse, and patted the earth beside her, inviting him to sit, as well.

He hesitated. "We should probably be getting back."

But they'd just called in when the cell signal allowed, and Bug had reported no major changes. His enzyme inhibitor had stabilized all of the nonviolent patients, though none showed signs of waking. Worse, their analysis of the creamer and tainted fruits and vegetables suggested that the poisoner hadn't isolated one or two proteins from the DLD fish—he'd done a wholesale protein isolation, effectively spraying the contaminated foods with atomized fish soup. Thom had sent the results off to the main lab, to see if they could do a subtraction and identify a second active ingredient, but it didn't look hopeful.

Until they got the results back, the lab investigation was pretty much at a standstill, which meant that Luke's theory of "find the bad guy, find the toxin" might be their last chance. Rox thought their best bet was looking at the Curse, and the players who might be affected by it. That was the reason she'd brought them to Beacon Lighthouse, where the Sea Captain's Curse had begun.

Luke had originally agreed to the plan. Now,

though, he looked ready to bolt, just as she had been that morning...and she thought she knew why. "Now who's afraid?" she said. "You don't want to understand this town and its inhabitants because you don't want to care about what happens next."

He bristled. "I care."

"You want to beat the disease. There's a difference." She patted the ground again. "Sit. This won't take long."

It was a foolish plan, she supposed, but she'd wanted to bring him to her favorite place in town, wanted him to see the wild beauty of the ocean. And yes, maybe she'd wanted him to look out on the waves crashing against the rocks guarding the harbor, and see the romance in the story.

He sat grudgingly, leaving a gap between them. "You said you were going to tell me about this curse, the one the people we met with today kept blaming for everything from the mayor's daughter dying on her wedding day, to the lack of tourists, to the outbreak, to...heck, everything."

Rox bristled at his attitude, but said, "Just sit for a minute. Listen."

He shrugged and did as she asked. As the quiet settled around them, they could hear the wash of the waves on the beaches below, the breakers crashing on the rocky promontory beyond the point where the lighthouse was built. The sky grew incrementally darker, and the clanging bells of harbor buoys set up a lonely-sounding ring.

After a few minutes, Luke shifted and sighed. "I'm sorry. I'm being a jerk because I don't want you to like it here. I want you to come back to D.C. with me."

Rox stiffened in surprise, not that he'd thought it, but that he'd said it aloud. "I'm—I'm flattered."

"That's not a 'yes.'" He paused. "But it's not a 'no,' either."

"We've done this before, Luke," she said softly. "It didn't work then and it won't work now—you said it yourself. Neither of us has changed."

"I'm based stateside now," he countered. "I even bought a condo."

Part of her wanted to be overjoyed at that bit of news, at the sign that he had evolved, after all. But he hadn't purchased a home because of her, because he was trying to compromise. It'd simply been the logical choice given his work.

She shook her head. "We're in a heck of a situation, being thrown together like this. Let's not make the residual attraction into more than it really is, okay?"

He was silent so long she thought he was going to argue, and part of her wished he would, wished he'd fight for her—fight for them—the way he hadn't before.

Instead, he finally nodded. "Okay. How about you tell me about this curse of yours?"

Reminding herself not to be hurt because he was doing what she'd asked, she swallowed hard, and began, "In the late seventeen hundreds, an English sea captain who'd amassed quite a fortune in a variety of not-very-nice ways knew the magistrates—and some of his victims—were closing in on him and his family. He bought a chunk of land in America and loaded up his wife and two small children, and they crossed the sea, headed for their new home. They almost made it, but got caught in a storm and wrecked right here."

As if punctuating her story, a huge wave broke over the rocky promontory with a terrible crash.

"The captain, Earl Raven, was the only survivor. Thinking that his sins had finally caught up to him, he dedicated himself to good deeds, vowing to never again let another ship wreck on this shore. He built Beacon Manor and the lighthouse, and manned the light himself while Raven's Cliff grew up around him. Eventually, he took on an apprentice, and when he died, left his entire estate to the apprentice with only one condition—the lighthouse was always to be lit on the anniversary of the death of his wife and children, and the light was to be shone on the rocks where they died."

"Let me guess, the apprentice and generations after him swear they see the ghosts of Earl and his family on those rocks when they shine the light on the anniversary." Luke waved a hand. "Sorry. Standard local myth, doesn't explain any of what's going on now."

"I haven't gotten to the Curse part," she said. "Legend said that the town would prosper as long as the descendants of the apprentice—the Sterling family—fulfilled the captain's one wish. And they always did—until five years ago when the heir, Nicholas Sterling the Third, forgot to shine the light on the rocks on the appointed day, and the lighthouse burned, killing his grandfather. That night, a category-five hurricane wiped out the town's fishing fleet and a good chunk of the buildings, and the townspeople have been struggling to rebuild ever since." She paused. "On the night of the hurricane, a woman disappeared and was presumed lost in the storm. Only recently, Captain Swanson learned that she was the Seaside Strangler's first victim."

"Which brings us more or less up to the present, but doesn't give us much in the way of leads on our poisoner."

"Maybe, maybe not." Rox frowned as things started turning over in her mind, loosened some by the story. "What if someone in town is using the Curse somehow, playing into it in an effort to cover up something bigger?"

"Like what?"

"It could be anything," she said, warming to the idea, which seemed so much more scientific than "it's just bad luck" or "Raven's Cliff is cursed." "What is it the cops say? Everything traces back to one of three things, money, power or revenge. So it could be political—maybe Mayor Wells is doing things to hurt the town so he can step in and save the day."

Luke shook his head. "You just don't like him. Granted, he's too slick, but I don't see it. I don't think he's got the guts to actually kill people. Besides, wouldn't he have saved the day by now?"

"Maybe." Rox frowned. "There are plenty of people who might want revenge, and more than enough bad blood to go around, given the troubles the town has been having. But they're all pretty specific cases. I can't see any of those people poisoning the entire town."

"Which brings us back to money, which is a heck of a motive," Luke mused. "But where's the economic upside to what's happening right now? Whatever got into those fish didn't kill them, it made them grow two, three times their normal size. That'd suggest someone trying to engineer the fishing industry to improve the catch, maybe combat hunger, that sort of thing."

"But the fish are inedible," Rox countered. "And while the first wave of DLD might be attributed to our mystery scientist doing some unauthorized testing, how do you explain the other victims? Why is he going after us, and why poison the other townspeople?"

He shook his head, frustrated. "Okay, the theory breaks down there. But it's something, anyway."

"That's true," Rox said, starting to see an avenue they could explore. "What about pulling the FDA licenses issued to any local researchers, and checking with chemical suppliers for purchases shipped to this area?"

Luke got a glint in his eye. "Exactly what I was just starting to think." He stood and held out his hand. "Come on, let's get on it."

"Sounds like a plan." She took his hand and let him pull her up, but when she moved to pass him and lead the way back to the SUV, he kept hold of her hand and tugged her back. She turned to face him. "What?"

He had a strange look on his face, far more open than she was used to, a little baffled, a little wistful. "This was good," he said. "You and me, bouncing off each other. I've missed that."

Telling herself to blame the film that crossed her vision on the incoming fog, she said, "That's twice now you've said something about missing me. Let me remind you, you're the one who left."

She was trying to pick a fight, trying to get them back on familiar ground when her heart wanted to bump in her chest and tell her it didn't matter what had happened in the past, what mattered was now, and how they went forward from here.

Only there was no now for them, she reminded herself. There was no forward.

Instead of taking up the argument, he said, "You were right, you know. I left because I couldn't handle seeing you in that hospital bed and knowing I couldn't do anything but stand there and watch. I couldn't fight the sickness for you, couldn't will you to get better."

Her throat tightened on the memory of waking up and finding him gone. "That would be the whole point of the 'in sickness and in health' clause. A relationship isn't always going to be two people raring to go."

"My father left when I was very little," he said, which didn't really address her point, but answered a whole lot of questions. "My mother raised me alone, and we did okay…until she got sick."

Rox reminded herself that this wasn't a surprise, that she'd suspected something of the sort. Still, her heart cracked a little and bled at the pain in his voice. "You watched her die."

He nodded, still holding her hand, but staring out to sea, where waves crashed on jagged rocks. "Yeah. Ever since then I've wanted to keep other people from dying, but I haven't been able to be around friends when they get sick because it reminds me of her. When you got sick…" He shrugged uncomfortably. "I was right back in that place, watching someone I loved die."

"I didn't die."

"You almost did."

She tightened her fingers on his, anger stirring. "So you figured you'd rather abandon me and break my heart than deal with the fact that you'd fallen for someone who was—hello—mortal? News flash. People die. It stinks and it isn't always fair, but it's a fact of life."

"I know." Now he turned back to her, his eyes gone a little cool. "And that's not really what happened. It was more that seeing you sick and thinking that you might die made me think about losing you. When you started to get better and we knew you were going to live, I was happy, but I was sad at the same time, because I knew that I was going to lose you anyway. We'd been fighting so much…I knew you were going to leave and come back to the States for good."

"So you left me before I could leave you," she said flatly. "Rather than talking to me about it, or seeing if we could work out a compromise."

"We'd been haranguing compromises for weeks, Roxie. They didn't exist—I wanted fieldwork and you wanted a home. End of story." He paused, and there was real regret in his voice when he said, "For what it's worth now, I'm truly sorry about the way I left. It was a knee-jerk, too-easy response and you deserved better. What we had deserved better."

"Yes, it did," she agreed, but when she looked for the relief she might've expected at finally getting it all out in the open, she didn't find it.

Rather, it seemed as though so many of the old resentments had already let go over the past few days as she'd worked beside Luke and rediscovered him, not as the ogre he'd become in her mind, but as the guy she'd fallen for, stubborn ego and all.

"Well," she said after a too-long moment spent staring at each other, holding hands. "We should go."

"Yeah. We should." But instead of releasing her hands he pulled her in close and folded her in his arms, buried his face in her hair and whispered, "I'm sorry."

The tears she'd been fighting for too long prickled at her eyelids. "Me, too." Because no matter how grievous his crime of leaving her in the hospital, he was right that their relationship had been on the skids long before then, and he hadn't been alone in creating the problems between them.

They clung together for a moment while the restless waters of the Atlantic washed up on the shores beneath Beacon Lighthouse and the buoy bells clanged in the harbor. The moment they should've pulled apart came and went, and neither of them moved, save to lean closer and melt into each other.

Rox felt her bones go liquid, felt their bodies line up, synch up, and told herself this was a really bad idea. But knowing it and doing something about it were two different things, and instead of pulling away, she found herself shifting, curling her fingers into the front of his shirt as his hands drifted down to her hips and dug in.

Then she eased away and he leaned in, and a kiss flowed naturally from that, as though they'd both known that was where they were headed, where they belonged. It started soft, a brush of lips, a question that had no answer.

Then Rox parted her lips on a sigh as warmth flowed through her, as heat built within her, as everything inside her eased on a sense of coming home.

"Luke," she said, just his name, and they parted by common accord, looking at each other, trying to figure out what came next.

"Back to the monastery?" he said, and he was asking about more than continuing the investigation.

"Back to the monastery," she said, not entirely sure what she was agreeing to, but positive she was tired of being alone.

AS HE DROVE THEM back to the monastery, Luke kept hold of Rox's hand and savored the unexpected lightness that had come with apologizing to her. He hadn't realized how much their parting—and his behavior—had weighed on him until it was out there in the open, hadn't realized how much he'd needed her forgiveness until he had it.

Granted, it came with a bit of sadness, too, as their conversation had only served to underscore that the differences that had divided them before—different goals, different speeds, different everything—divided them still. But at the same time, she seemed willing to act on the attraction if the time seemed right, willing to take the days they had left together, stealing precious hours together amidst the strain of work and medicine, as they had once done.

Ignoring the faint warning chime at the base of his brain that said he might not have been as clear as he could've been about that whole "using the time we have left" concept, he parked the SUV in front of the monastery.

"Let's do this," he said, and climbed out of the car. He was anxious to get going on their new theory of a rogue scientist at work, and equally anxious to finish for the day and get started on their other new theory: the two of them together, if only temporarily.

Seeming equally motivated, Rox joined him on the stairs headed up to the main entrance. They were halfway up when there was a motion from the shrubs to one side.

"Rox, get back!" Luke shouted, spinning to cover her as a man leaped onto the stairs, putting himself between them and the door.

His eyes glowed red.

Chapter Ten

Luke pulled the .22 he'd made a habit of carrying, and leveled it at the Violent. "Don't be stupid. We can help you."

But the man didn't attack. He held up both hands, which trembled as though he was palsied. His voice was muffled and his mouth worked strangely when he said, "I won't…hurt you. I've come to…help." He reeled back and fell, sagging against the door, clearly weak from the disease, and loss of blood.

He was wearing a torn white rag it took Luke a moment to identify as a lab coat. When he made the connection, a burn of excitement took root in his gut.

"Luke," Roxie said from behind him. "He could be the scientist we're looking for."

"I'm his lab assistant," the man said, voice hitching on his shallow, panting breaths. "I'm sorry…. So sorry. Thought we were doing…good. Ending world hunger. Sorry, sorry, sorry…" He devolved to a babbling sing-song of apology.

Luke pocketed the gun and stepped forward to grab the guy by the lapels and give him a shake. "Can you stand? Let's get you inside. We've got an experimental therapy that should buy you some time."

The man shook his head. "Nothing can...help me now. He didn't give me...the extracted proteins. When I said...wouldn't be a part of it anymore...he injected me with the fish nutrient...which is...fatal within an hour. Then he...threw me out and...left me to die."

Luke and Rox crouched closer as his voice faded. "What nutrient?" she demanded. "Do you know how to counter it?"

He nodded. Wincing, he reached into his mouth and pulled out a wad of something. "Crazy bastard didn't think to search...in there." He pressed the soggy mess into Luke's hand. "Save them...town shouldn't have to suffer..."

He trailed off, going limp.

"Wait!" Rox said quickly, urgently. "Who is *he?* Who did you work for?"

But it was too late. He was gone.

Luke stood. "Godspeed, stranger. Thank you for doing the right thing." He turned to Rox, holding out his hand, where the wad of paper sat, saliva-soaked and leaking ink. "Let's see what he died to bring us."

MAYOR WELLS'S fingers trembled as he punched in the phone number he'd hoped never to use, and waited for the other man to pick up.

"This isn't a good time," his investor said brusquely, not bothering with a hello.

"You told me to call if the doctors started getting close to the FDA licenses and chemical purchases." Wells clutched the handset, which had gone slippery with sweat. "They're making the calls now. They know everything."

The other man cursed, low and bitter. "Okay. I'll deal with it."

"Do you want me to—" Wells began.

"No. Stay out of it." The line went dead.

Wells put down the phone, but he didn't leave his office to join Beatrice for another silent, strained dinner he wouldn't taste. Instead, he rose and reached for his briefcase, popping the clasp and withdrawing the unregistered weapon he'd carried for days now.

Yes, his investor had told him to stay out of the way, probably to protect him in case things went wrong. But Wells couldn't help thinking of the points he'd gain if he helped his mysterious friend.

Maybe even enough to make that senate seat a reality.

"Sorry, folks," the mayor whispered. "It's about priorities."

He left through a side door. Beatrice probably wouldn't even notice he was gone.

"CAN YOU READ IT?" Rox was practically vibrating with impatience as she leaned over Luke's shoulder, watching him unfold the page on the kitchen table. "Can we make the antidote here?"

He scanned the page—it was legible, thankfully—and mentally reviewed what they had on hand. Then he nodded. "It'll be a slow process, but yeah, we can do it. Lucky for us we brought in so many reagents for the hybridizations."

Thom stared at the schematics, his lips working silently. After a minute, he said, "Yeah. We can do it."

"Then let's get started."

Captain Swanson leaned against the kitchen table, arms crossed, expression pensive. "You're sure he didn't tell you anything about where he came from?"

Rox shook her head. "Positive. He just kept talking about being sorry, and wanting to bring us the cure. Do you recognize him?"

Swanson shook his head. "He's not a local, that's for sure."

They were all gathered in the big monastery kitchen—Luke and his teammates, Roxie, the police chief and two of his officers. The doctors were concentrating on the antidote, though Luke was keeping half his attention on the cops.

Provided they could make the antidote, they should be able to cure the outbreak and get Raven's Cliff headed in the right direction again, but that still left the question of who had developed the fish nutrient in the first place.

It wasn't even really a nutrient, he thought, looking at the first of the chemical structures on the page, that of the original molecule. It looked more like some of the cancer chemotherapeutic drugs, only this one created at least one mutation that they were aware of, and probably more.

Worse, according to the stranger, it was highly toxic to humans.

"Why would someone want this thing kicking around?" Rox said, leaning over his shoulder again. "Any scientist in his or her right mind would've shut this project down long ago."

"The key words being 'in his or her right mind,'" Luke agreed. "Since he appears to have taken this 'nutrient' straight from the bench into open-ocean testing, I think we can agree sanity and ethics aren't his top priority."

Swanson pushed away from the table. "Well, you two have certainly given us some good leads to work with. I'll see what I can do about tracking down drug purchases and FDA licenses coming into this area."

"Let me know if you need me to throw my weight around at all," Luke offered. He glanced at the laptop screen and noted the time. "Though I doubt either of us is going to get very far before business hours tomorrow."

"True enough." The police chief sketched a wave and headed out, leaving two officers to stand guard.

"I'll pull together some dinner," Rox offered.

Luke nodded. "Sounds good, I'll help Bug and—"

He was cut off by the sound of gunfire from the front of the building, followed by a man's yell.

"Stay here!" Luke shouted, and headed for the front at a run, pulling his .22 as he ran.

Rox was right behind him. "Captain Swanson, are you okay?"

Luke snarled, "I told you to stay in the kitchen, damn it!" But as she'd reminded him the night before, he wasn't her boss. He cursed under his breath. "At least stay the hell behind me."

He peered around the arched door leading to the entryway. "Patrick? You okay?"

"I'm okay," Swanson called. He stepped through the main doors, looking disgusted. "He didn't even come close to hitting me."

Luke said, "I take it he got away?"

"Yeah, damn it all. Bastard was in the tree line, just waiting for someone to come through the door. He got off a couple of shots, hit a window upstairs, I think, and took off. Between the dark and the fog, I couldn't stay on him."

Rox stepped around Luke. "Do you want help searching?"

Before Luke could say something to the effect of "no way in hell are you wandering around in those woods with someone out to kill you," Swanson said, "With all due respect, Doc, that's probably not a good idea. I'll put a couple more officers on duty here for the overnight, and we'll have a look around in the morning."

Luke was forced to acknowledge—inwardly, at least—that the police chief got the point across with far more tact than he would've used.

"Come on." Luke took Rox's arm and tugged her away from the main door. "Let's not be targets. Besides, we've got work to do."

But it turned out over the next few hours that preparing the antidote took very little work and a great deal of waiting around for chemical reactions to occur.

"Can't we speed this up?" Rox asked. "What if we increase the incubation temperature a little?"

But Bug shook his head. "Sorry. You know what Luke always says."

She grimaced. "Yeah. Science takes the time it takes, blah, blah."

"Right. You want a guesstimate? The first few doses of the antidote won't be ready until morning."

"If that's the case—" she stretched, yawning pointedly "—I'm going to catch a few hours. Wake me if you need me for anything."

Luke tried not to read too much into her words— they hadn't made any promises to each other down by the lighthouse, and a great deal had happened in the interim to totally kill the mood and bring them back to the reality of the deadly outbreak.

Then she paused at the doorway, angled her body so the others couldn't see, and sent him a look that was about as come-hither as a look could get.

His body went on high alert in an instant.

Play it cool, he told himself. *Don't be too obvious.* He didn't want her to feel like anything between them was right out in the open, didn't want her awkward around Bug and Thom if there was even a prayer that she'd consider rejoining his team.

He'd made the offer on the spur of the moment, but the more he'd kicked it around in the back of his brain, the more perfect it seemed. It was the compromise she'd wanted before—she'd have a home base in D.C. that she could nest however she wanted, while he could keep doing his work as a field responder.

And they'd have their nights together.

Body humming at the thought, at her blatant invitation, he shifted and very carefully *didn't* look toward the door.

"Would you just go already?" Bug said from his computer station, and Thom snorted agreement without looking away from his chemical preparation.

Luke thought about playing it innocent, but didn't figure that'd get him far. So instead he chucked all thought of subtlety. "Holler if anything happens."

And headed for the room he'd shared the night before with Roxie, this time hoping to share a bed.

ROX TOLD HERSELF there was no reason to be nervous. He'd either come or he wouldn't, they'd make love or they wouldn't, and none of it would matter in the long run. This was a moment out of time, an aberration, a stolen flashback.

They knew they were good together, and after their frank talk at the lighthouse, they knew where they stood with each other. This was just two people who'd missed each other's bodies, nothing more.

And if her heart ached a little at the thought, and her stomach fisted on a moment of grief when the doorknob turned and the panel swung inward, she was the only one who needed to know it.

Then he was standing there, letting the door swing shut at his back, and his eyes were on her, dark and hazel and intent, and there wasn't any room for sadness inside her.

There was simply desire.

"Roxie," he said, only her name, but the single word was rough with desire, with a timbre that caressed her nerve endings and set her aflame.

She crossed to him, skirting the piles of her things jammed into the narrow space between the cots, her eyes locked on his. She didn't say a word. There had already been plenty of talking between them—more, perhaps than there should have been.

Instead, she placed her palms flat on the hard planes of his chest, feeling the warmth and muscle beneath the tough material of his shirt, feeling his sharp inhalation and the steady drum of his heart. Curling her fingers into his shirt, using the grip as leverage, she stretched up high on her toes, and touched her lips to his.

As earlier, the kiss started soft, only this time there was no hesitation, no question...and his response left no doubt that they were on the same page.

He groaned at the back of his throat, the sound harsh with longing, and his arms came up to band around her, holding her close with more fervor than grace, as though he was afraid she might change her mind.

But she loved the feel of his rough, possessive grip, and the taste of him, hard and masculine and edged with need. There was no thought of candlelight or soft words, no promises needed between them, there was only the heat that slapped at her, speared through her and spiraled high, urging her on.

Yes, her body said. *Yes, him. Luke.*

It had always been Luke for her, still was. She refused to think about a future without him because them being together wasn't about the future, it was about right now, about taking what they both wanted in the moment because, as she'd learned all too well over the past week, the future wasn't certain.

Terrible things could happen to good people with no rhyme or reason, life could change in an instant. She'd known that before, of course—she'd seen people die, seen families torn apart—but this was personal. It was her town, her people. And in struggling to care for the people she'd claimed as her responsibility, she'd learned something about herself, too.

She needed to take what she wanted, because nobody was going to walk up and hand it to her.

So she took, pouring herself into the kiss, rising up on her toes to press her breasts against his chest, wedging herself more and more surely against him, into him.

His hands shaped her body, kneaded her flesh, sending up starburst sensations everywhere they touched. She moaned, arching against him, asking without words for more. Demanding more.

He swept her up in his arms and carried her the few paces to one of the cots—his, hers, it didn't matter. It was a flat, yielding surface for him to lay her on, then follow her down.

With so little room on the narrow bed there wasn't much space for them to draw apart, but they didn't need it. They twined together, kissing and touching, and fitting together perfectly, one to the other.

She unbuttoned his shirt and ran her hands beneath, finding the same ticklish spots, the same faint scars across his shoulders and back, along with a newer, ridged scar just below his hairline. She hesitated at it, but didn't ask. Tonight wasn't about knowing each other, it was about having each other.

He kissed her avidly, hungrily, as he drew her shirt up and off, and dispatched her bra with a practiced flick he'd once claimed to have learned in high school.

That remembered detail sent a sharp slice through her, the information made more poignant by what she now knew about that time in his life, when he'd watched his mother fading from her disease and vowed to do what he could to prevent other families from being ripped apart.

She thought of the young man he'd been as she kissed his throat, and the hollow beneath his ear, thought of the man she'd known as she ran her hands along his taut chest and the lean lines of his abdominal muscles. But as he turned his head once again and their lips met in a kiss, it wasn't the young man he'd been or the one she'd known before that she was kissing. It was the man she'd relearned over the past days under the worst of circumstances.

A man she liked and respected. A man she could've

loved had the situation been different. Had *they* been different.

She murmured her pleasure as he cupped her breasts in his hands and worked her, stroked her, bringing her close to the peak with the clever flick of his thumbs, though she was still wearing her jeans.

Heat suffused her, overwhelmed her, and the jeans were suddenly too much, the barriers between them too much. She eased aside and worked herself free, then waited while he shed the rest of his clothes and quickly located a condom in the suitcase she vowed to never again call too organized.

Then he was back with her, stretching atop her, twining around her, his grip strong and demanding in passion.

There would be time later—perhaps—for more subtlety, for more creativity, but for this time, this first and maybe only time, she wanted to touch him from nose to toes, wanted the good, solid weight of him atop her, within her.

She spread her legs at his urging, wrapped her thighs around him and skimmed her feet along his calves. He slid his long, hard shaft against her, teasing her, making sure she was ready when she was well beyond it.

Then, finally, too soon and yet too long in coming, he slid inside her on a long, strong thrust that stretched her, filled her, made her remember the sense of being complete.

Tears touched the corners of her eyes and she dashed them away because this was no time for tears. It was time to slide her arms around his neck and hold on for the ride, for the pleasure.

"Roxie," he said again, and this time she said his name in response, whispering it into his ear.

They moved together, barely moving at all, riding the long, slow wave of pleasure that came at the feel of him flexing within her, delving ever deeper until he was seated to the hilt, his body pressed up against her sensitized flesh, rubbing ever so slightly.

He framed her face in his hands and kissed her as they looked into each other's eyes and she saw herself reflected in the hazel depths, and felt the warmth they made together.

Pleasure coiled on a long, slow throb that pulled at her core, as her inner muscles caressed the hard flesh within her. He groaned long and low and quickened the tempo just right, and they moved together, long-time lovers who knew how to touch each other, how to complete each other, in the bedroom at least.

The heat gathered and spread, prickling small fires everywhere her skin touched his, and Rox moved beneath him, urging him onward, driving him higher and harder.

His breath rasped in her ear, sending shivers down the back of her neck, and she scraped her fingernails lightly across the ticklish spots, making him shudder and buck against her.

They hung on to each other, clung to each other as their bodies gained in rhythm. Blood sang hard and hot in her veins and the fiery pleasure of him, the surge of him inside her, against her, tightened her to a greedy throb of muscle and sensation. Beyond himself now, he drove into her again and again, his head thrown back, his control lost, given to her as a gift of trust.

And it was that trust that sent her over the edge, the

knowledge that they were both bare to each other, holding nothing back as he thrust into her and cut loose with a roar.

They came together, clung together, cried out together, and then held each other as the pleasure crested and ebbed. Even after it was done and their bodies cooled and their breathing leveled out, they held each other, unspeaking.

When they finally broke apart, when Luke eased off of her and stood, it was only to kill the light and drag the other cot closer so they could fall asleep, intertwined.

Complete.

ACROSS TOWN, the mayor and his wife were also in bed, but there was no twining going on. Beatrice snored softly in tranquilized bliss while Wells sat on the edge of the bed, anticipating the call, yet fearing it at the same time.

"I helped him out," he told himself. "Swanson was going to call on the licenses. I diverted him, distracted him."

Still, when the phone rang, he jumped and his pulse skyrocketed as he grabbed for the receiver. "I can explain. It was all part of a plan to—"

"Stop talking," the mechanized voice interrupted. "I need you to do something for me."

"What?"

"Sell the lighthouse."

"Excuse me?" For a second he thought it was a joke, something those crackpot townies had cooked up, the ones who thought their troubles were all because the lighthouse wasn't working and the dreaded sea captain was exacting his revenge.

As far as they were concerned, he should sell Beacon Manor and the lighthouse—two of the biggest historical landmarks in town—to Teddy Fisher, the eccentric businessman who'd promised to restore the lighthouse to its former glory.

"Right," he said, seriously annoyed. "Like I don't have more important things to worry about right now. Tell me why I should care about the damn lighthouse."

"Because I have your daughter."

The five simple words went through Wells like lightning. He was pretty sure he actually felt his heart stop, then start up again, banging in his chest as though it was going to explode. "You—you found her body?"

"Not her body. Her. She's alive."

"Oh, dear God." Wells sank into himself, sagging to the bed and sliding off the edge until he was sitting on the floor with his knees to his chest and the phone clutched to his ear.

Logic said there was no way this guy—whoever he was—had Camille. But logic could take a flying leap as far as he was concerned. If there was even the slimmest possibility of seeing his little girl again...

"Do you want her back?" the robot voice asked.

"Yes!" he practically shouted, and then when Beatrice stirred above him on the bed he dropped his voice to a whisper. "Yes, of course. Tell me what to do."

"I already did. Sell the lighthouse or she dies."

THE THICK FOG had gone nearly to a drizzle by the time the Seaside Strangler was ready with his preparations. The sacrifice needed to be done quickly and his Sea

Bride was already unconscious, so he had decided to dispense with his usual ritual of drugs and indoctrination.

Instead, he brought with him the gown she would need, along with the seashell necklace he would use to perform the sacrifice.

Her boat waited in a secure location, not yet prepared. Once the sacrifice was complete, he would bring her to the skiff and secure her with seaweed before setting her adrift, straight into the riptide. Holes in the bottom of the craft would send her to the sea gods, and the town would be saved.

Bolstered on wings of religious fervor, he barely felt his feet on the stones of the narrow pathway along the cliff side, leading to the secret cave where he'd put her after the sea gods had led him to their chosen. He was whistling softly when he stepped inside the long, narrow entryway. Pausing to light the oil lantern in honor of Captain Raven, he moved along the narrow passage leading to his bride.

But she wasn't there.

The ropes he'd used to bind her lay coiled on the cave floor, neatly untied, indicating that this was the right cave, but his bride had fled.

Rage suffused him. He flung back his head and roared his denial and disdain for the bitch who hadn't appreciated what he was trying to do for her, for all of them.

"Get back here!" he cried, his words echoing in the interconnected cave system. But there was no answer, no sign that there was anyone else in the caves besides him.

She'd escaped, the bitch.

The wind must've picked up outside, because there was suddenly a hollow keening sound in the tunnels, the whip of air moving through crevices in the rock above.

"The gods," he murmured, remembering what had happened the last time the sea gods became angry, when they had wrecked half the fishing fleet in a single night. "The gods must be appeased."

He turned and retraced his steps, back up the cliff face and toward the ruined lighthouse. The wind tugged at his hair and clothes, the sea gods reminding him that they would not be denied.

Just when he thought the gods were going to punish him for losing their chosen one, he heard voices.

Girls' voices.

Snuffing out the lantern with a quick, practiced puff, he stashed his supplies in a crevice between two rocks and eased toward the sound, which was coming from the lighthouse.

"Shh," one girl said. "The chief extended the curfew for the prom, but we're still way past it. Keep it quiet, will you?"

"Who's going to hear us?" a second girl said. "The captain's ghost?" She laughed as she said it, and a tendril of wind howled through as the gods screamed their dislike of her mockery.

"Thank you, sea gods," he whispered, knowing they had let the other woman go so he would be drawn to these girls instead. Taken together, at their entry to adulthood, they would be strong enough to avert the plague, strong enough to save the town.

Bowing his head in prayer, he kissed the seashell necklace he would use to cut the breath away from them.

Then he stepped out from concealment and claimed his brides as the wind howled its approval and the sea crashed on the rocks below.

MILES AWAY, in the mansion he'd purchased upon his return to town, the recluse felt a cold, oily shiver crawl down his spine. He imagined a choked-off scream and saw a flash of white, then nothing.

He didn't know why or how he knew, but he was quite positive that in that moment, something truly terrible had happened out by the lighthouse.

Chapter Eleven

Rox awoke just before dawn, feeling warm, sated and well-loved, and when she opened her eyes, she found Luke propped up on an elbow, watching her.

She almost pulled the sheet up to cover her breasts, but didn't because there was something so achingly tender in his expression that she felt cherished instead of embarrassed. So she blinked at him, and smiled. "Good morning."

"Yeah." He leaned in and touched his lips to hers. "It is."

Seeing that he was fully dressed, she said, "Status check?"

"Bug gave May the antidote about twenty minutes ago. Assuming it works, we've got enough for two others, so we'll dose Jeff and Wendy, who were the first to get sick. Then we'll call around to see who else we can put on making the stuff. If the area hospitals will pitch in and help us make the antidote, then we'll be able to speed up production."

"The closest hospital is forty minutes or so away," she said. "But you're right, every bit will help." She paused. "Has the chief had any luck finding the missing Violent, or checking on those chemical purchases?"

He shook his head. "There's been no sign of Doug, and it's still too early for the companies to be open. Besides, Swanson is thinking he should go the warrant route and make sure it's all nice and legal before he starts calling. Whoever this guy is, he's well-funded and smart. No sense in leaving him a legal loophole."

Now she did pull the sheet up, and shifted to sit, wrapping the bedclothes around her, not because she was feeling self-conscious, but because she realized, all of a sudden, that they were talking about the mop-up work.

Assuming the antidote worked, Luke's job in Raven's Cliff was done.

"You're leaving," she said, the words coming out more like an accusation than she'd intended.

He sat up so they were eye-to-eye, sitting cross-legged on the dragged-together cots. He took her hands and held them. "*We're* leaving, Rox. I meant what I said yesterday—I want you back on my team. I've got a base of operations in D.C., which I didn't have before. We can stay in my condo and you can work the in-lab end of the team business or come out into the field. Totally your call." Apparently taking her stunned silence for shock, he grinned. "It's exactly the sort of compromise you wanted before."

And the worst part was, Rox realized, he actually believed what he was saying. "No," she said, feeling an awful, yawning gulf open up inside her. "Luke, no."

She saw a flash of something in his eyes that suggested he wasn't as oblivious as he seemed, but he said, "You don't want to move right into the condo, that's fine. We can rent you a place of your own while we find our balance together again." He squeezed her hand in his. "What matters is that we're back together."

"No," she said again, and pulled her hand from his. "And that means 'no' to all of it, Luke. We're not back together. I'm not going anywhere. I like it in Raven's Cliff. I'm making a home here."

"But this..." He gestured between the two of them, and the bed. "Us. How can you walk away from it?"

"The same way you did," she said bluntly, though it was tearing her up inside. She wanted to rail at him for being a stubborn, egotistical ass who thought that compromise was the same as convenience, for not offering to give up as much as he was trying to take away from her. "You were right all along. Nothing's changed."

She stood, taking the sheet with her, and maneuvered awkwardly to dress beneath it, while he sat on his cot, confusion giving way to anger.

"You're picking this town and these people over what we could have together?" he finally asked, seeming incredulous, offended.

She nodded and sniffed back a tear, and her voice hitched a little when she said, "The same way you're picking your career over me yet again."

"It's not the same at all," he said, anger lacing over a faint hint of "you've got to be kidding me." "You're a town doctor in a messed-up place that doesn't appreciate you, and I'm—" He broke off, apparently seeing the danger too late. "I'm sorry, I didn't mean that the way it came out."

"Yes, you did." Clad in her jeans and bra, she wadded up the sheet and tossed it on her cot, trying not to smell their mingled scent in the close confines of the narrow room, trying not to remember the feel of him against her in the night, the perfection that the two of them had found together, in bed but not in real life.

He was silent for a moment, then said, "Why Raven's Cliff?" He sounded truly baffled.

She sighed, feeling like they were right back where they'd been two years earlier. "Because whether they like me or not right now, they need me. And when I was a kid, back before the lighthouse burned and the town was prosperous and happy, they made me feel welcome. My father was a salesman with a habit of selling more than he could deliver, which meant we moved around a lot. We lasted almost two years here in Raven's Cliff, I think because the police chief—the man Patrick replaced—kept tabs on my dad and stopped things from getting too out of hand. Eventually they did, of course, but before that, the people here tried to help my mother, and they were kind to me."

She shook her head. "I don't remember their names or faces—all the towns sort of ran together after a while—but I remembered that the years we spent in Raven's Cliff were the happiest, and safest-feeling times of my childhood. I want to pay that forward now."

"It's a different town now, Rox. The people are different. You don't owe them anything."

As the afterglow of a perfect night finished draining to the imperfection of daylight, Rox felt empty and hollow. Her bones ached, her heart hurt. "It's not the town, Luke. It's us. The things we want from life are too damned different."

"Now who's not compromising?" he snapped. "I'm offering to meet you halfway."

"No," she said firmly. "You're not. You're offering to give me what's easy. That's not the same."

His expression had gone hard and stubborn. "I don't understand you when you get like this. I never did."

"Exactly." She headed for the door. "Lucky for us we figured that out before we got married, or heaven help us, had kids." She turned back with her hand on the doorknob, and it pained her soul to see him sitting there, looking lost. "You've got a great life, Luke. You've got everything you ever said you wanted."

"Do you?" he asked.

Her heart turned over in her chest a little at the simple question, and the fact that he truly cared about her answer despite it all. She smiled sadly. "I'm working on it."

Figuring that was as good an exit line as she was likely to get—and knowing she had to escape before she broke down entirely—she pushed through the door and let it swing shut at her back.

The hallway was deserted, though there seemed to be some sort of commotion coming from the front of the monastery, by the main doors. Frowning, she headed in that direction. She hadn't gotten more than a few steps when a doorway flew open and a red-eyed man lunged at her, hands outstretched.

Rox reeled back, opened her mouth to scream—

And everything went dark.

ONCE THE DOOR had closed at Rox's back and he'd heard a couple of bangs, like she'd kicked a doorway or two on her way to the kitchen, Luke sat alone in the narrow stone room, trying to figure out how that had gone so wrong, so quickly.

He'd thought he had it all figured out. She wanted a home, so he'd offered his own. She didn't want to travel, so he'd come up with a way for her to stay behind when the rest of the team went off on assignment. He wasn't the one refusing to compromise, he thought on a rising burn of anger. She was.

But beneath the anger was a hollow echo of loss, of failure, and it was the failure that cut the deepest.

You can do anything you want to do, be anything you want to be, his mother used to tell him, her voice thready and nasal from the oxygen feed. *You're going to succeed. You're going to be a winner.*

And he was. He was at the top of his field, the go-to guy. He saved lives, not just one or two at a time, but by the dozens. The hundreds. How could Rox possibly think what she was doing now was as important as that? And what did she want from him?

It didn't seem like she wanted a damn thing, he realized, which rankled. She hadn't asked him to quit his job and stay in Raven's Cliff. She accused him of wanting everything his way, but in the end she was the same. It was her way or the highway.

Well, apparently it was going to be the highway. Again. And this time he'd leave with everything having been said between them. He wasn't running, he was saying goodbye to an unworkable situation. At this point, it was better to do it sooner than later. He needed to get out into the field lab, get more doses of the antidote processed and the patients on the mend and get the hell out of Raven's Cliff.

This time, he wouldn't look back.

Cursing, he shoved to his feet and crossed the room, kicking some of her stuff out of the way. It wasn't until he reached the door and cracked open the heavy panel that he heard the buzz of angry conversation. Lots of it, in unfamiliar voices.

Adrenaline jolting, Luke yanked open the thick door. He took one look at the crowd of healthy townspeople arguing in the hallway, caught sight of Thom at the back of the crush, looking harried, and bellowed, "What the *hell* is going on here?"

The noise level dropped for a second as the townspeople turned to look at him, then the clamor redoubled as they recognized him and pressed forward, shouting pleas and threats.

"My Joshua is just a baby," one woman said, grabbing Luke's hand in supplication. "Please. You've got to save him!"

A heavyset man in a boat-logo ball cap jostled her out of the way. "Rosie!" he shouted. "You've got to give it to Rosie!"

Six other people lunged toward Luke with similar demands, and all he could think was, *Oh, hell. This is going to get ugly.*

Somehow—from one of the cops, from someone trying to stir up trouble, he didn't know—the families had found out that the doctors in the monastery had an antidote, but only in limited quantities.

"Quiet!" he shouted, raising his hands over his head and waving them, trying to cut through the din. "Everybody be quiet. Please!"

Thom had managed to work his way through the crush, and bent close to say, "Watch what you promise them. The patients we stabilized with the anti-CP 12.21 are starting to crash again."

Luke cursed. That was going to put them in a race

to produce enough antidote before more people died. It also meant they were going to have to prioritize who got treated first.

And they needed to do it without the family members breathing down their necks.

"Okay, people," he said, making shushing motions as the crowd quieted. "Let's settle down here." Out of the corner of his mouth, he muttered to Thom, "Get Swanson and his men here, stat."

"They're on their way."

"And the antidote?" Luke asked, though what he was really asking about was May.

That brought a lightening of Thom's expression. "She's responding. It's too soon to tell for sure, but it looks good. Bug is with her now."

"That's something, anyway." It was way more than "something," but the sudden pressure in Luke's throat wouldn't let him get much more out. Relief flared at the thought that he hadn't totally failed May, that she might make it, after all.

When the people nearest him started to shift and mutter, he returned his attention to crowd control. "Here's the deal, folks," he said, pitching his voice to carry. "We have uncovered a treatment that appears to be successful in counteracting the effects of Dark Line Disease—what you've been calling the Curse. At this moment, we are making the drug as quickly as possible, and we're contacting local hospitals for help with production."

Under normal circumstances he might not have laid out the situation quite that frankly, but he had a feeling most—if not all of them—already knew that much.

"Who gets treated first?" a man in the back called,

and the question was picked up in several other voices.

"The sickest patients," Luke answered simply, which got him an equal mix of glowers and nods.

A quick head count showed that there were twenty or thirty people crowded in the hallway, and probably twice that in the entryway. *Too many,* Luke thought, and hoped to hell Swanson got there soon.

"Where are the four cops who were supposed to be standing guard?" he asked Thom.

The biochemist looked around, and frowned. "Good question. Maybe the crowd took them out when they got through the doors? I don't know, I came running when I heard the commotion. I called Swanson first thing, then tried to get to your room and warn you." He glanced past, into the sleeping room. "Where's Roxanne?"

Luke's gut iced in an instant. "She's not with Bug?"

"I haven't seen her," Thom said, face blanking to worry. "Do you think—"

The squeal of a bullhorn interrupted him, and Captain Swanson appeared at the back of the mob with close to a dozen officers behind him. "Listen up," the chief barked, his voice fuzzed and amplified by the bullhorn. "The best way for you to help your friends and family right now is to go the hell home and let the doctors do their jobs."

At first, Luke didn't think it was going to work, as the mob shifted and its members glared at him and Thom, and at the cops who started moving among them, speaking in low, stern tones and starting to herd people toward the front door. But gradually the crowd in the hall thinned as people started moving toward the entryway and stalled there, eddying near the closed front doors.

Luke didn't pay much attention to that, though. Figuring Swanson had the crowd in hand, he started pushing his way through, heading for the kitchen. "Roxie," he called. "Roxanne!"

"I'll look in the patients' rooms," Thom called, and headed in the opposite direction.

"What's wrong?" Swanson called, lowering the bullhorn as Luke struggled past.

He didn't answer, just kept going. *She's in the kitchen brewing tea,* he told himself, but deep down inside he knew that didn't make sense. She would've been in the thick of things the moment she heard the commotion. She wasn't the kind to hide and wait for danger to pass.

That knowledge pressed on his chest and weighed on his soul as he scanned the kitchen—empty—and headed back the way he'd come, shouting, "Roxie, answer me!"

She couldn't have left the monastery, because she would've run across the mob and been swept up in the melee on her way out. Which meant she was missing, along with the four cops who should've been stationed in the hallway.

And that gave Luke a very bad feeling.

"Captain Swanson!" he called. "We've got a problem!"

At that moment, a heavyset man over by the main doors shouted, "They're locked!" He rattled the knob, then threw his weight against the heavy panel. "Someone's blocked us in!"

Luke met Swanson's eyes, and saw his own dawning horror reflected in the police chief's expression.

The mob had been a setup, a way to entice more inhabitants of Raven's Cliff out to the monastery. Now they were all going to be trapped in the stone building together, at the mercy of the shadowy figure who wanted the doctors dead and the mystery of his "nutrient" unsolved.

And somehow, somewhere, the bastard had Roxanne.

"Try the back!" Luke shouted, waving toward the kitchen. "There's another door!"

The crowd surged in that direction, but Luke headed the other way. He stuck his head in May's room. "I want you to lock all the patients' rooms," he told Bug, who was wide-eyed with fear. "Then get back in here and shut yourself in with May. Don't let anything happen to her."

Bug nodded. He held out a pair of loaded syringes. "Thom told me to keep these, but I think you should take them. You could need them more than me."

It was all that was left of the first batch of the antidote.

Luke nodded, and pocketed the syringes. "Thanks."

Then he went, not to the room he'd shared so briefly with Roxie, but to the room she'd stayed in the first night, the one with the column in the corner.

The moment he was inside, he heard the heavy tread of footsteps, coming not from the hallway, or from the walls, but from the floor beneath him. The footsteps were dragging and uneven, warning that they belonged to the missing Violent, or others like him.

Rox had been right about the secret tunnels, he realized. She'd just been wrong about where they were located.

Cursing, fearing that he was already too late, he dragged the cot away from the wall and started looking for the trapdoor he knew had to be there.

ROX AWOKE IN a narrow stone space, and for a moment she thought she was in the room that she and Luke had shared. But the air was stale and there was no natural light, only the glow from bare lightbulbs strung at wide intervals along a long, low corridor.

She was in one of the monastery's secret passageways, she realized with a jolt. But how? Why?

"Good," a man's muffled voice said from behind her. "You're awake."

She turned to look at him, and realized she was tied, her hands and feet bound together behind her, so her every move strained her shoulders and hips.

Her captor stood over her wearing a lab coat over casual clothes, and a ski mask concealing his face. Behind the mask, his gray eyes gleamed with mad satisfaction.

Panic flared hard and hot, and she opened her mouth to scream.

"Don't." He shoved a wad of cotton floss in her mouth and taped it in place with a strip of adhesive while she thrashed and gargled, trying to make a sound, any sound that would bring rescue.

"Luke," she screamed behind the gag. *"Luke!"* But all that came out was a weak, terrified whimper.

"You should've gotten sick right away," the man said thoughtfully, as though to himself. "I sprayed the coffee in your clinic with the extract, after all. But, no. You had to make things difficult, and by the time I realized you were going to be a problem, the others were already here." He tsked as though she were a naughty child who deserved punishment, and pulled a syringe from the pocket of his lab coat. "Now we've got a real mess on our hands, and I have to clean it up."

He uncapped the needle and pushed through a drop of the clear liquid within the syringe, as though it really mattered whether or not he gave her an air embolism.

Seeing the fear in her eyes and hearing her muffled cry of alarm, he smiled. "Yes, poor Jason warned you before he died, didn't he? My former lab tech is quite correct—the nutrient triggers incredibly fast growth in fish, and equally fast death in humans. Which is why my new investors are so excited about the possibilities of using it as a bioweapon...and why I can't allow you or your friends to jeopardize our plans."

Rox cringed and tried to squirm away as he advanced on her, but he got a foot across her neck, holding her down like she was some sort of animal as he stuck the needle in her upper arm and depressed the plunger.

The injection was a cool burn followed by a faint tingle that dissipated within seconds, but Rox's heart shuddered in her chest at the knowledge of what would come next: fever and malaise, then the reddish eyes and body sweats. Then death.

The antidote was designed to cure humans who had eaten the contaminated fish or proteins extracted from those fish, not the nutrient itself. They had no idea if it would work on the actual toxin.

She was going to die.

Hopeless, helpless tears filmed her vision as the masked man straightened away from her and tossed the syringe carelessly aside. Then he leaned down to whisper in her ear, "Don't worry, you won't be alone for long. Your boyfriend and his buddies, the cops and a good chunk of the town are trapped in this building with you. I'm going to send my little army in after them, and once they're all inside, wham!" He clapped his hands together, making her flinch. "I'll seal the place and pump it full of a special gas I've been working on. Everyone will just fall asleep, and bye-bye." He paused, his voice going reflective. "Then…I'll simply disappear. Even with you gone, there are too many people on the outside who'll be looking for me and trying to steal my greatest invention. I need time to work on it, to perfect it."

The world grayed out for a moment as he gave her a fond-seeming pat, as though she were a lab rat. A test subject.

Then he strode away, the tails of his white coat swinging as he walked, looking for all the world like a hotshot doctor striding along the hospital corridors.

At the thought of her own hotshot doctor, Rox's tears broke free and tracked down her cheeks. She hated that their last words had been in anger, hated even more that he'd struck a chord in their fight.

He'd accused her of not being willing to compromise, either, and he'd had a point. She hadn't offered a solution, had only shot down his suggestion, not because she didn't want to be with him, but because she wanted it to be on her terms for a change. So much of their time together had been spent doing what he loved, wasn't it fair that she got to do the same?

Perhaps, but she'd needed to say that to him. And maybe she'd needed to give a little, too. There had to be a compromise where they both gave up something, both gained something. But instead of figuring out where that middle ground might lie, she'd jumped down his throat and they'd fallen right back into old, pointless patterns.

Now it was too late to go back and try again.

Her tears dripped down her chin and landed on the stone floor beneath her as she cried for herself, for Luke. For the hints of perfection they'd both been too stubborn to make a life out of, and the fact that they wouldn't get another chance to try.

And that, she realized with a start, was giving up. Which was the same thing as running away. How could she expect Luke to fight for her if she wasn't willing to do the same?

She might be dying, but she would damn well make her last few minutes on earth count.

So, as the sweat of a fever broke out across her body in the first stage of the toxin's effects, she worked her mouth beneath the adhesive until the tape came loose, and she was able to push it off with her shoulder.

Afraid to shout for help because she could hear the tramp of dragging footsteps and the screams that suggested the Violents were already loose within the monastery, she rolled over, squirming, making her joints howl in protest as she angled her bound hands around to the front of her body.

Then she went to work on the knots, tugging with her teeth, refusing to give up until the last moment, when her heart stopped beating and it was truly over.

HEARING ONE OF the Violents drag-stepping along the narrow secret passageway toward him, Luke beat a hasty retreat to the last corner he'd rounded, where a waist-high, unlit offshoot passage gave him a hiding place.

Just in time, too. He'd barely ducked in and scrambled back, out of the light, when the Violent shuffled past.

Luke was just edging out into the main tunnel when he heard a low-voiced conversation and froze.

"I left those four guards in the antechamber below the main doors," a man's voice said, sounding well-modulated and clear. "Once you and the others have secured the people on the main level, bring the cops up to join them. I want everyone in one place for the gas."

"Yesssh," a second man said in the slurred voice of an end-stage Violent, followed by the sound of the two men moving off in different directions.

Gas, Luke thought with dawning horror. He froze, jammed between what he knew he should do, and what his heart was telling him to do. He should double back and return to the main floor, and try to free Swanson and the other cops to help him search the secret passageways, find the mad scientist and neutralize him and the Violents before the gas attack began.

But the insistent pound in his blood told him to find Roxie first, a gut-level conviction that she needed him right away. *She's my top priority,* he thought, and the realization gave him pause.

He'd never told her that before. He probably hadn't shown her enough, either, which was why she'd constantly accused him of putting his job first, of choosing his career over her.

But he could control the job to a point, he realized. He couldn't control her, or his feelings for her. She made him crazy, made him worry that she'd leave him, that she'd die, that he'd fail her somehow.

And that was it, he knew with sudden, panicked clarity. His insistence on short-term assignments and short-term affairs wasn't about being afraid to care, afraid to love. It wasn't even about being afraid to watch someone die, though that was part of it.

He was petrified of failing.

He handed off assignments that looked unsolvable, bailed on relationships that got too complicated, avoided May when her case started looking hopeless. He wasn't a success because he was a top-notch doctor. He was a success because he only fought battles he thought he could win.

Well, that stopped now. He didn't intend to fail Roxie, but he wasn't going to win by walking away this time. He was damn well going to find her, and he was going to do his best to save her. Maybe he'd fail, but at least he would've tried.

Cursing, he darted back into the main passageway and started running in the direction he thought the scientist had come from, calling her name in a whisper. "Roxie? Rox, can you hear me?"

His heart thudded against his ribs and banged in his ears, nearly drowning out her answer when it came.

"Luke!"

He bolted toward the sound of her voice, relief pouring through him when he saw her up ahead, lying prone and bound, but moving. Alive.

He dropped to his knees beside her and started yanking at her bonds. "I'm here, Rox. I've got you. Everything's going to be—" *Okay,* he was about to say, but broke off when he turned her over.

Her skin was flushed and sallow, her eyes red with more than tears.

Chapter Twelve

"Oh, Roxie." Luke's voice went rough on her name.

"I'm sorry," she whispered, and clung to him. "I'm sorry for everything."

"Me, too." He kissed her, and felt her fever as his own.

Grief hammered at him. Panic. Self-recrimination. If only he'd been faster to find the trapdoor at the base of the pillar, or found her sooner once he was in the secret passageways.

"Wait!" He scrabbled in his pocket, came up with the syringes. "I have the last two doses of the antidote."

She grabbed his wrist before he could pop one of the caps off. "Don't. He injected me with the toxin itself. The antidote won't work."

"We don't know that for sure," he said urgently. "We have to try." Before she could object again, he injected her, hoping against hope that the antidote to DLD would at least slow down the destructive cascades the nutrient had triggered in her body.

Her breathing grew labored, until it rattled in her lungs. She grabbed at him, eyes going wild. "He's going to barricade everyone in and fill this place with gas. You have to stop him!"

Luke cursed bitterly. He didn't have time to be a hero. He needed to help Rox. It stood to reason that at least some of the secret passageways led outside the monastery. If he carried her outside, to fresh air—

She'd still be dying of the nutrient, and the madman would have won by killing the others.

If he stayed with her, he was failing Bug, Thom, May and the residents of Raven's Cliff. But if he went after the scientist, he'd be failing Rox and the wonderful things they could have together.

"I'm not going to let you down, Roxie," he said urgently. "I love you. I'm sticking by you."

Her reddened eyes glowed, not with violence, but with emotion. "I love you, too. But you need to leave." The glow faded. "I'm sorry, Luke. So sorry."

She went limp in his arms...but she was still breathing, and her eyes were open.

There was still time for him to help her, Luke thought, mind racing. But how? She was limp and nonresponsive, but her eyes were open.... Exactly, he realized with a jolt, like the earlier patients had done in the later stages of the DLD.

And Bug's anti-CP 12.21 treatment had altered that status.

"I'm not giving up on you, Rox." He gathered her in his arms and lifted her, carrying her through the passageways back to the trapdoor through which he'd entered.

He paused below the trapdoor, and listened for footsteps from above. Hearing none, he hoisted himself up a set of inset stone handholds and cracked the door, scanning floor-level for any company in the small room.

Finding the coast clear, he popped the hatch and lifted Rox through, then followed her up. He closed the trapdoor, gathered Rox against his chest and carried her across the room. He still didn't hear any footsteps, and when he cracked the heavy wooden door and looked out, he found the hallway ominously clear.

The mad scientist had told the Violents to gather everyone in the entryway. It seemed as though the townspeople and patients had already been herded to their destination—leaving the west wing of the monastery deserted.

Moving as silently as possible, Luke ghosted across the hall, to the supply room. He didn't think he could make it to the field lab in the kitchen wing—not with the Violents and their captives in the entryway. But he and the other doctors had left doses of certain drugs— tranquilizers, anesthetics and the like—in the supply room, in a small case secured with a combination lock.

He closed and locked the door, which would provide a warning if not much protection. The Violents had already proven they could break through the heavy doors if they wanted to. Then he placed Rox on the floor, trying not to panic at her utter stillness and the faint gray cast that was overtaking her skin, indicating that her circulatory system was starting to shut down.

Holding his breath and crossing his fingers that Bug had loaded doses of the anti-CP 12.21 into the lock box, he keyed in the combination and snapped the case open.

The original antidote was there.

Exhaling on a rush of relief, a flare of hope, he snatched up the preloaded syringe and went to his knees beside Rox. It took him a tense minute to get her vein to plump, further sign that her circulation was faltering.

When he finally got a vein, he slid the needle in and backed the plunger to draw the dark red blood into the syringe, confirming that he was in the vein.

Then he held his breath, and injected the anti-CP 12.21 into her bloodstream.

And prayed.

ONE MINUTE Rox was floating, and there was only warmth and numbness around her. In the next, there was roaring pain.

She jolted, her eyes flew open, and she arched, screaming. Seconds later, a big hand clapped over her mouth and Luke was in her face, hissing, "Shh. They can't hear us! Shh, hush, Rox. I'm here. I've got you. I'm here." He kept repeating the words, over and over, holding her close, rocking her, soothing her.

Being there for her.

Rox bit her lip to keep the cries inside as the pain washed over her, through her, seeming to take over everything. Eventually, though, after what seemed like forever but was probably only a minute or two, the pain faded to discomfort, then to pins and needles. Then it was gone.

"Oh, boy." Rox exhaled a shaky breath and pressed her face to his chest. "Oh, God. What just happened?" But even as she asked the question, she remembered the tunnels, and the masked man. Luke injecting her with the antidote, and her being sure it wouldn't work.

"I'm alive," she whispered, shifting to look up at him. "How?"

He smiled slightly, and she saw herself reflected in his eyes. "Teamwork. Bug reverse-engineered his original treatment based on the genetic change caused by the nutrient. I'm betting if we do a few tests, we'll find the nutrient doesn't cause mutations in humans, it directly targets other systems. But Bug's molecule was close enough to the DNA target in the fish that the nutrient glommed right on, neutralizing both of them." He lifted a shoulder. "It's a theory, anyway."

She looked around, realizing they were in the supply room. "You carried me all that way?"

"I would've carried you as far as it took," he said simply, and for the first time in their roller coaster of a relationship, she believed it, believed she could count on him to be there no matter what came between them, whether it be location, careers, fights…or the threat of death.

She didn't even realize she was crying until he wiped the tears from her cheeks. She gave a watery sniff. "Thanks for the rescue. You're my hero."

He shook his head. "You saved me first, by reminding me that being a hotshot and a hero doesn't matter worth squat unless you have someone to share it with."

There were tears in his eyes, as well, but she realized with sudden dawning horror that it wasn't because of emotion.

She sniffed again, and this time got a whiff of something nasty. "The gas," she said fearfully. "He's started pumping it in. We don't have much time, we have to do something!"

"We will." He squeezed her hands and stood, tugging her up with him. "Grab as many surgical masks as you can, and layer them over your nose and mouth, and bring extras with us."

She did as he said, her heart pounding painfully in her chest as the air got increasingly stale. Luke grabbed a heavy metal rack and swung it at the barred window. The glass shattered with a crash and the air got lighter.

Then, suddenly, she heard pounding footsteps in the hallway, screams of panic, and slurred shouts of rage.

Luke's face went grim. "The Violents must've realized our scientist doesn't intend to let them out. They're all looking for an exit, but he's blocked them off."

Rox shivered. "What about the tunnels?"

"I'm betting the Violents will go into survival mode once they get a lungful of the gas and panic. They'll forget all about the tunnels and hammer at the ground-level doors. They're not very bright at the end-stage."

"Can we get out through the tunnels and stop the gas?"

He shook his head. "I don't know the way out. We need a guide." He handed her a syringe full of a clear liquid. "Be ready."

She didn't have a chance to ask "ready for what?" because seconds later he yanked open the door and shouted, "Hey!"

Several townspeople ran past, screaming, but it was the big, hulking figure of a Violent, all red eyes and temper, that filled the doorway.

Rox screamed and backpedaled as she recognized Doug Allen, the man who'd killed the chef and his assistant at the Italian restaurant.

Roaring, Doug lunged toward her. Luke slammed

and locked the door, then spun and leaped on the Violent's back, driving the other man to the floor.

"Inject him!" Luke gasped as Doug jackknifed beneath him, fighting for freedom. "Quick!"

Rox leaped forward, popped the protective cap and plunged the needle into the big man's upper arm. She pushed the drug in, and withdrew the needle as the Violent roared and bucked.

Seeing that Luke was losing his grip, she got Doug's flailing arms up behind his back and applied leverage, trying to keep him under control. He howled and thrashed with superhuman strength, nearly pulling away from them twice.

After maybe a minute his struggles slowed. Then they ceased.

Then he drew a long, shuddering breath and exhaled on a long moan. "Oh, my God. What have I done?"

It sounded like a normal man's voice.

Luke and Rox exchanged looks. At Luke's nod, she let go of her grip on Doug's hands and stepped back. After an assessing pause, Luke levered himself off the other man and helped him roll over.

Doug's eyes were reddened with gas and tears, but not with disease. He looked from Luke to her and back, and his features crumpled. "I *killed* them." He rolled onto his side and put his face in his hands, repeating it over and over again. "I killed them. I can't believe I killed them."

"Doug!" Rox bent near him and pulled at his hands. "Doug, I need you to listen to me. We need your help, quickly! There are many more people in danger and you can help them. Are you listening to me? You can save lives if you help us now."

But Doug wasn't listening, he was howling his grief, his body bowed in an arc of disbelief. "I killed them!"

"Quiet him down," Luke ordered. "Someone's going to hear."

But it was already too late. Stagger-stepping footsteps drew near out in the hallway, and heavy blows made the doorway shudder as another Violent started pounding on it. "Let me in!" roared the Violent. "In!"

Panic surged through Rox. They were trapped in a dead-end room with bars on the windows and a Violent at the door.

"Keep talking to him," Luke ordered, heading for the window with purposeful intent, as though he knew something she didn't.

Even with the window broken open the air was starting to get thick in the supply room, and Rox's head spun. "Doug," she said urgently. "You've got to help us get out of here! The man who made you sick is going to kill a lot of people if you don't. But if you help us, it'll make up part way for what you've done. You were sick, Doug. You didn't know what you were doing." She patted his shoulder. "You didn't know."

Finally, he quieted and went still. Pulling his hands from his grief-stained face, he said thickly, "What do you need me to do?"

The door splintered and gave beneath the blows of the Violent out in the hallway. He'd be inside the room any moment.

"Show us the way out," Luke said. Rox gasped with relief when she saw that he stood next to a carved

pillar in the corner of the room, holding up a stone slab
to reveal access to the tunnel system below.

Doug nodded. "I think I can do that."

WELLS STUMBLED through the forest for a second time,
this time in daylight. His hands were sweaty and kept
slipping on the grip of his revolver.

How had things gotten so out of hand so quickly?
He'd had everything under control, moving smoothly
in the right direction. Then that bitch of an aide had
gotten wind of the kickbacks, and he'd been forced to
pay her off. The man on the phone had *not* been happy
about that. He'd been even less amused that the investigation was headed exactly where he was supposed to
make sure it didn't.

"Fix it," he'd said, "or I'll fix you."

But amidst all the bad news was the great, glorious,
wonderful news that Camille was alive, that she'd be
released the next day, once he'd finalized the sale of
Beacon Manor.

Beside that, most everything else faded. But not
really, because he couldn't enjoy having Camille back—
and his wife out of mourning—if he was dead. Ergo, he
had to take care of his problem in the monastery.

But when he got there, he found that someone had
already beaten him to it, and with a far more elegant
solution.

ROX FOLLOWED DOUG through the tunnels, with Luke
right behind her. She was woozy and light-headed
from gas as well as the rapid-fire injections of the
nutrient followed by the two antidotes, but she was on
her feet and moving.

"The door is up here," Doug said. "Just around the next corner."

"Let's switch places," Luke said. "If the bastard is out there, I'm in better condition to fight."

They made the change, with Rox squeezing close to the wall so the men could pass. Luke touched her hand on the way past, bringing a warm glow to her heart, though one that was tempered with caution as reality intruded. It was all well and good to exchange I-love-yous in the heat of the moment, when they were both just grateful to be alive. It was quite another to make it work in the day-to-day grind, and she already knew Luke excelled at the grand gestures but fell far short when it came to the daily business of life.

When they reached the stone panel that the cured Violent said would lead to the outside, Luke gestured for her and Doug to move off to one side. Then he felt around for the trigger mechanism, and cracked the door to reconnoiter.

"It looks clear," he whispered a moment later. "And I see the mechanism that's pumping the gas into the monastery."

"Is the scientist there?" she whispered back.

"I don't see him." Luke paused. "Stay here. I'm going to take a look, and shut the pump down. I'll reverse it if I can, see if I can get some circulation going to dissipate the gas as quickly as possible. Wait until I give you the all's clear."

Rox nodded, but her insides churned with nerves. "Be careful."

He leaned in for a quick, hard kiss. "You, too."

Then he was gone. Rox held her breath and stood in the rocky doorway, which opened around the side of the monastery, and was disguised as a piece of the huge structure's granite foundation.

Behind her, she heard Doug groan and slide down to sit on the floor of the tunnel, propped up against the wall. She heartily wished she could do the same, but she stayed strong for Luke, and for the patients and their families, who were depending on them to shut down the gas.

Luke crossed the grassy verge beside the foundation of the big building, staying low. When he reached a whirring generator attached to a series of pipes and bottles, he crouched down and fiddled with the mechanism.

Moments later the motor noise stopped, then after a pause, it started up again at a different pitch. Luke turned and waved to Rox. "Got it. All clear!"

She gave a glad cry and burst from concealment, racing toward him with her arms outstretched. "We did it!"

She was halfway across the open space separating them when a shot cracked out from the nearby forest.

"Down!" Luke shouted, and Rox hit the deck. He sprinted to her, dropped down beside her, feeling for injuries. "Are you hurt?"

"No," she said, shoving him away. "He missed. Get the bastard!"

He was gone in a flash, bolting into the trees, heedless when two more shots rang out, going wild. Then he roared a primal battle cry and flung himself on a man who had broken cover behind a scrubby bush and turned to run.

Rox struggled to her feet, calling, "Doug! Get the main doors open and drag the police officers out, then shut the doors again. Once they're awake, help them contain the other Violents. We'll need more antidote before we can let them go free!"

Then she was off across the grass, limping toward where Luke and the other man had disappeared.

She came upon them in a clearing just in time to see Luke get the bastard by the scruff of the neck and slam him to the ground face-first. Luke's face was bruised and battered, and already starting to swell, but she loved the lean lines of it, and the determination when he whipped the other man's arm up behind his back so high his captive howled with pain.

"I didn't do it!" the other man shouted. "It's me. Percy Wells. I came to help, I swear!"

Luke cursed and flipped the mayor over, but didn't back down. "Then why did you shoot at us?"

Wells held up both hands, the gun having fallen free in the struggle. "I'm sorry, I'm sorry. I thought you were him, the man who started the generator. I saw him one minute, then the next he was gone. Then you were there, and I panicked." He was close to blubbering now, and there was no mistaking the fear in his eyes. His voice dropped to a broken whisper. "I was only trying to help, I swear."

Luke looked across the clearing at her. "What do you think?"

"Let Swanson have him," she said, swaying a little on her feet. "He'll figure everything out."

Luke frowned. "Rox? Are you okay?"

"Nuh...no." The sway became a lurch, and suddenly the world was spinning. "I don't feel so good. I think...I think all the injections are catching up to me."

She pitched to the ground as the world went gray. The

last thing she knew was the feel of strong arms holding her, and the sound of Luke's voice whispering, "Don't worry, Roxie. I've got you, and this time I'm not letting go."

As RAVEN'S CLIFF seethed with news of the near tragedy up at the monastery and the doctors' heroic rescue of their patients and other townspeople—as well as the lady doctor's collapse just thereafter, and rumors of the mayor's involvement—the well-dressed scientist took the opportunity to slip along the cliff-side pathway to the caves hidden beneath Beacon Lighthouse.

The mayor had made the deal and sold off the lighthouse, which meant it was up to him to hold up his end of the bargain, by returning Camille to her father.

His other plans might not have gone as well as he'd hoped, but this one was right on schedule.

Whistling softly, the scientist picked his way through the cave system, using his flashlight to light the way. When he reached the cave at the far end, he stopped dead, the whistle dying on his lips.

She was gone.

Unable to believe his eyes, he strode into the chamber and circled the small space, cursing, trying to figure out what had happened. She'd been there two days earlier, had still been unconscious. Had she come around and somehow managed to escape?

No, he thought. *Impossible.* Even if she'd regained consciousness, she'd been securely chained. The old shackles were easy to open from above, but it would've been impossible for her to unchain herself. Which meant someone else must have rescued her.

Or maybe not a rescue per se, he realized. If she'd

been rescued—or escaped—she would've turned up in town by now. Someone else had taken her, stealing his prize.

The scientist thought quickly. He could search for her, but there was no guarantee she was still in the cave system, and he couldn't very well call the cops or go door-to-door and ask if anyone had seen the mayor's dead daughter. But at the same time, he'd made a deal. If he double-crossed Wells, there was a chance the mayor would reveal the bargains they'd struck, and involve the cops, maybe even the feds.

Unless...

A smile touched the mad scientist's lips as he thought of a way to use the recent chaos in Raven's Cliff to his advantage.

Chapter Thirteen

In the days following Luke and Rox's harrowing escape from the monastery, she drifted in and out of consciousness. She was alternately burning with fever and wracked with chills as her body responded to the agents she'd been injected with.

Her white cell count was off the charts, her hormone levels were haywire and when she did wake, she wasn't terribly lucid. But against all odds she was alive, and her body was fighting hard to clear the foreign substances and return her to the land of the living.

Through it all, Luke stayed at her bedside. He wanted her to see him every time she woke, wanted her to hear his voice telling her she was going to get better, that he was there for her, that he loved her. Not just that, but he wanted to be beside her through the illness. He needed to be there, needed to watch her breathe, watch the drip of the IV that fed fluids into her body, guarding against dehydration.

Bug and Thom had helped him move her to her private apartment over the clinic, so she wouldn't have to be in the monastery anymore. They had stayed on in the monastery, helping a second team of doctors manage the Violents, and prepare and administer the antidote to all the remaining patients.

The patients' recoveries following administration of the antidote were nothing short of remarkable. Some, like May, took a few hours to respond, while others, like Doug, recovered almost immediately. The one common denominator was that all of the DLD sufferers who survived to receive the antidote made a full recovery, both Violents and non-violents.

Still, the town mourned the lost. Mr. Prentiss and his older son went home without the other two members of their family, and Mary Wylde would raise her two children without their father, Henry. Doug Allen teetered on the brink of depression over the people he'd killed, and the Raven's Cliff cemetery would gain six new headstones.

And that wasn't the end of the troubles in Raven's Cliff, either. Though Mayor Wells protested his innocence, loudly and in great detail to anyone who would listen, Captain Swanson had uncovered evidence that the mayor had been the mastermind behind production of the deadly nutrient. In the midst of the furor *that* announcement had caused came more tragic news when the bodies of two young women washed up on the beaches south of Raven's Cliff. Identified as high school seniors Cora MacDonald and Sophia Lagios, the girls had last been seen the night of the prom.

The police, including Sophia's brother, homicide detective Andrei Lagios, were keeping the details quiet, but rumor said the girls had been found wearing white dresses and seashell necklaces, indicating that they had been the victims of the Seaside Strangler.

The curse, it seemed, had not yet left Raven's Cliff. And as far as Luke was concerned, he wasn't leaving until it did...and maybe not even then, if Rox would have him. So he sat by her bedside, fielding increasingly irate calls from his higher-ups as they learned how free and loose he'd played with regulations, dosing numerous patients with thoroughly unapproved drugs.

At first he listened and apologized, because his bosses were right—the rules existed to protect the patients, and he'd skirted way too close to the "harm" side of the "do no harm" part of the Hippocratic oath. But after a while, he got sick of the bureaucratic garbage and snapped, "It worked, didn't it? What would you rather have me do, let them all die?"

"You got lucky," his boss's boss said.

"I know," Luke replied, glancing over at Rox's sleeping form and feeling a tug of love, and the worry that went with caring.

"Unofficially, I agree with everything you did," his boss's boss admitted. "Officially, though, you're suspended pending an investigation into your actions."

And though a year ago—heck, a couple of weeks ago—that would've been devastating news, now Luke turned away from the bed and shrugged. "Good. Saves me from requesting a leave of absence for the next few months."

He rang off soon after, and in the silence that followed, Rox said, "You're staying?"

He looked at the bed, and his chest tightened when he saw that she was awake, her eyes clear and bright. "Yeah," he said, voice thick with emotion. "I am."

ROX STARED AT HIM, assessing, not quite daring to believe he was saying what she hoped he was saying. He'd said he loved her, had said they'd make it work. And he'd stayed through her illness; every time she'd opened her eyes he'd been there, making her feel cherished and safe.

But still, she'd made assumptions about him before and gotten burned.

"For how long?" she said now, even though deep down inside she knew there wasn't a right answer to the question. If he said he was leaving as soon as she was back on her feet, he'd break her heart again. But if he said he was staying for good, how could she be sure she believed him?

He shook his head. "I'm not sure. Definitely until things have settled down in this town of yours."

Sitting down in the chair beside her bed, he took her hand in one of his, and used his free hand to brush her hair away from her face, tucking it behind her ear in a gesture so tender it brought tears to her eyes. "Then you're not really staying, are you?" she whispered.

"I think that's something we should decide together," he said, leaning in so he could look into her eyes. "There's going to be two of us from now on, maybe more later, when the time's right to start a family. So I foresee some serious negotiations in the future, like whether we both live here full time, or we split our time between here and D.C., or whatever. And you know what? I don't really care where we live and what we do, as long as we're doing it together."

Her gathered tears brimmed up and spilled over as she realized she'd been wrong before. Apparently there was a right answer to her question, and that was it.

They'd figure it out together.

Feeling her strength return on a wash of love and trust, she reached across and slid the IV from her vein, wincing slightly at the burn. Then she levered herself up in the bed and reached for Luke.

He met her halfway and held her hard, and she could feel all the love and worry and stress in his big frame. "Thank you for staying," she whispered, pressing her face into his chest.

He pulled away and grinned down at her. "Just try and get rid of me, I dare you. I'm in it for the long haul this time, whatever it takes." He paused. "I love you."

"Love you back." She grinned and lifted her face to his, and they met in a kiss that closed one chapter of their lives and began another. As they kissed, twining together like two halves of a whole, a gentle summer breeze blew through the open window of her bedroom. On it she heard the cry of a seagull and the clang of a harbor buoy, and she realized that Raven's Cliff might be a home, but Luke—and their love for each other—was her center. It had taken them some time to find their way back to each other, but now that they had, she was finally at home in his arms, and in his heart.

And she was going to stay there, forever.

* * * * *

The trouble isn't over yet. Don't miss
the next installment of this spine-tingling new series,
THE CURSE OF RAVEN'S CLIFF,
when Cassie Miles presents
IN THE MANOR WITH THE MILLIONAIRE,
only from Harlequin Intrigue!

The editors at Harlequin Blaze have never been afraid to push the limits—tempting readers with the forbidden, whetting their appetites with a wide variety of story lines. But now we're breaking the final barrier—the time barrier.

In July, watch for BOUND TO PLEASE by fan favorite Hope Tarr, Harlequin Blaze's first ever historical romance—a story that's truly Blaze-worthy in every sense.

Here's a sneak peek...

BRIANNA stretched out beside Ewan, languid as a cat, and promptly fell asleep. Midday sunshine streamed into the chamber, bathing her lovely, long-limbed body in golden light, the sea-scented breeze wafting inside to dry the damp red-gold tendrils curling about her flushed face. Propping himself up on one elbow, Ewan slid his gaze over her. She looked beautiful and whole, satisfied and sated, and altogether happier than he had so far seen her. A slight smile curved her beautiful lips as though she must be in the midst of a lovely dream. She'd molded her lush, lovely body to his and laid her head in the curve of his shoulder and settled in to sleep beside him. For the longest while he lay there turned toward her, content to watch her sleep, at near perfect peace.

Not wholly perfect, for she had yet to answer his marriage proposal. Still, she wanted to make a baby with him, and Ewan no longer viewed her plan as the travesty he once had. He wanted children—sons to carry on after him, though a bonny little daughter with flame-colored hair would be nice, too. But he also wanted more than to simply plant his seed and be on his way. He wanted to lie beside Brianna night upon night as she increased, rub soothing unguents into the swell of her belly, knead the ache from her back and make slow, gentle love to her. He wanted to hold his newly born child in his arms and look down into Brianna's tired but radiant face and blot the perspiration from her brow and be a husband to her in every way.

He gave her a gentle nudge. "Brie?"

"Hmmm?"

She rolled onto her side and he captured her against his chest. One arm wrapped about her waist, he bent to her ear and asked, "Do you think we might have just made a baby?"

Her eyes remained closed, but he felt her tense against him. "I don't know. We'll have to wait and see."

He stroked his hand over the flat plane of her belly. "You're so small and tight it's hard to imagine you increasing."

"All women increase no matter how large or small they start out. I may not grow big as a croft, but I'll be big enough, though I have hopes I may not waddle like a duck, at least not too badly."

The reference to his fair-day teasing was not lost on him. He grinned. "Brianna MacLeod grown so large she must sit still for once in her life. I'll need the proof of my own eyes to believe it."

Despite their banter, he felt his spirits dip. Assuming they were so blessed, he wouldn't have the chance to see her thus. By then he would be long gone, restored to his clan according to the sad bargain they'd struck. He opened his mouth to ask her to marry him again and then clamped it closed, not wanting to spoil the moment, but the unspoken words weighed like a millstone on his heart.

The damnable bargain they'd struck was proving to be a devil's pact indeed.

* * * * *

Will these two star-crossed lovers
find their sexily-ever-after?
Find out in
BOUND TO PLEASE
by Hope Tarr,
available in July wherever
Harlequin® Blaze™
books are sold.

Harlequin Blaze marks new territory with its first historical novel!

For years readers have trusted the Harlequin Blaze series to entertain them with a variety of stories— Now Blaze is breaking down the final barrier— the time barrier!

Welcome to Blaze Historicals—all the sexiness you love in a Blaze novel, all the adventure of a historical romance. It's the best of both worlds!

Don't miss the first book in this exciting new miniseries:

BOUND TO PLEASE
by Hope Tarr

New laird Brianna MacLeod knows she can't protect her land or her people without a man by her side. So what else can she do—she kidnaps one! Only, she doesn't expect to find herself the one enslaved....

Available in July wherever Harlequin books are sold.

HARLEQUIN *Super Romance*

Lawyer Audrey Lincoln has sworn off
love, throwing herself into her work
instead. When she meets a much younger
cop named Ryan Mercedes, all her logic
is tossed out the window, and Ryan is
determined that he will not let the issue
of age come between them. It is not until
a tragic case involving an innocent child
threatens to tear them apart that Ryan
and Audrey must fight for a way to
finally be together....

Look for

TRUSTING RYAN
by Tara Taylor Quinn

*Available July
wherever you buy books.*

HARLEQUIN
More Than Words

"I have never felt more needed as a physician…"

—**Dr. Ricki Robinson,** real-life heroine

*Dr. Ricki Robinson is a Harlequin More Than Words award winner and an **Autism Speaks** volunteer.*

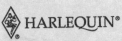

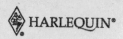
HARLEQUIN®

INTRIGUE®

COMING NEXT MONTH

#1071 IDENTITY UNKNOWN by Debra Webb
Colby Agency
Sande Williams woke up in the morgue—left for dead, her identity stolen.
Only Colby agent Patrick O'Brien can set Sande's life straight, but at what
cost does their partnership come?

#1072 SOLDIER CAGED by Rebecca York
43 Light Street
Kept under surveillence in a secret, military bunker, Jonah Baker is a
damaged war hero looking for a way out. Sophia Rhodes may be the one
doctor he can bend to his will, but their escape is only the first step in
stopping this dangerous charade.

#1073 ARMED AND DEVASTATING by Julie Miller
The Precinct: Brotherhood of the Badge
Det. Atticus Kincaid knows more about solving crimes than charming
ladies. But he'll do whatever it takes—even turn quiet Brooke Hansford
into an irresistible investigator—to solve a very personal murder case, no
matter the family secrets it unearths.

#1074 IN THE MANOR WITH THE MILLIONAIRE
by Cassie Miles
The Curse of Raven's Cliff
Madeline Douglas always had dreams of living in the big house. But taking
up residence in historic Beacon Manor is the stuff of nightmares, which
only the powerful and handsome Blake Monroe can help to overcome.

#1075 QUESTIONING THE HEIRESS by Delores Fossen
The Silver Star of Texas: Cantara Hills Investigation
With three murder victims among her social circle, Caroline Stallings isn't
getting invited to many San Antonio events. Texas Ranger Egan Caldwell is
the one man returning her calls, only he's spearheading an investigation that
may uncover a shared dark past.

#1076 THE LAWMAN'S SECRET SON by Alice Sharpe
Skye Brother Babies
Brady Skye was a disgraced cop working tirelessly to win back his
reputation. But only the son he never knew he had can help him piece
together his life—and reunite him with his first love, Lara Kirk—before
someone takes an eye for an eye.